Secrets

Secrets

C.A Dalton

To order additional copies of this book, contact:
Xlibris Corporation
1-888-795-4274
www.Xlibris.com
Orders@Xlibris.com
66558

This book is dedicated to my adoring husband who has supported me in every endeavor I have undertaken, especially writing this book and to Kim for helping me realize it is OK to talk about secrets and how I have many stories in my head just waiting to be told.

Acknowledgments

This book wouldn't be possible without the help of several people. The encouragement and support from my husband and children helped me keep the dream alive that yes, I too can be a published author. My publishing consultant, whom I consider a good friend, was invaluable. Renn, it was your encouragement that kept me going, through the difficult moments, in writing this book. My baby sister was my unofficial "editor"—Ami, you're the best! Rebekah and her best friend, Traci, for their wonderful help in note writing/ texting lingo and allowing me to use their handwriting.

Thank you girls! I <3 you! I also need to acknowledge my good friend Mark. Not only has Mark been there for me when we built our house, but he was there supporting me with this book and giving me helpful hints along the way. And last, but not the least, my students who were aware that I was writing this book and encouraged me in ways they will never know. Thank you, everyone!

Chapter 1

As the wind howled through the trees and whistled through the cracks around the window of her bedroom, Felicia sat curled in a ball in the corner of her bed. She hated nights like these; nights that were so dark that one couldn't see two feet in front of them with the wind making it even eerier. Curled up in her ball, she held tightly to her favorite stuffed animal, trying to find solace and comfort. She winced at the thought of any of her friends finding her like this. Everyone at school thought of her as someone who was quiet, yet very confident. What a joke that was. Her extreme fear of nights like this was proof that she amounted to nothing more than a big baby.

"How did I end up like this tonight?" Felicia wondered out loud. What started out as a perfectly good day quickly turned to a night that filled her with fear.

Felicia looked at her bedroom clock and saw that the time was glowing the indigo blue numbers of 1:30 a.m. She groaned at the thought of having to get up early to go to school in the morning, but couldn't bring herself to leave her position on her bed. Even though she had finally reached the grown-up age of seventeen, stormy nights sent her back to her childhood fears of storms. What she couldn't understand, though, was why the fear seemed to increase as she became older. As she sat on her bed, rocking and clinging to her favorite stuffed bear, she decided to read a bit from the latest book she checked out of the library, hoping it would help calm her; she had a big geometry test that day and needed some sleep.

A loud buzzing sound slowly penetrated through the fog of Felicia's sleep. Abruptly, she sat up as she realized the buzzing noise was her alarm clock. She pushed her curly, red hair out of her eyes and crawled out of bed. As she reached for the alarm clock, she looked out the window and saw small tree limbs and leaves littered across the yard. Felicia shivered as she remembered the fierceness of the storm that kept her awake most of the night. She glanced at the book lying on her bed and figured she must have fallen asleep while reading.

At least that was something that helped, she thought to herself. *Now, what to wear to school today?* As she pondered, on which outfit she heard her cell phone buzz with a text message, it was from her best friend, Celia.

"Hey, wats up? Wat r u wearing today?" Celia asked.

"Not sure yet. Probably just jeans and T-shirt." Felicia sent back.

"OMG! Did u catch that storm last night? Wasn't it awsum??"

Felicia sighed. She was not into storms like Celia was. Personally, she would rather not be reminded of it, but she couldn't tell Celia that. Even her best friend had no clue what a big baby she was.

"Yeah, I heard it. Look, I got to go. I'll catch ya at school."

And with that, Felicia grabbed her clothes and headed to the bathroom, dreading the day to come. She had yet to study for the geometry test that she had to take during the fifth hour. *Can this day get any worse?* Felicia thought as she began her morning routine.

~*~*~*~*~*~*~*~*~

Felicia ran into school as the last bell rang for the first hour. She discovered that yes, the day could get worse. The traffic into town was a nightmare and took her longer to get to school than normal. It didn't help that she had to drive her dad's old clunker to school. It barely did forty miles per hour on a good day. *I wish my parents would let me get a car for myself. I hate only being allowed to use this car to and from school.* Felicia thought to herself. There went studying for the geometry test before school started. When would she learn to start studying *before* an hour or two prior to the test? *Never!* snorted a voice in her head.

Felicia slid into her desk as Mrs. Harmon began the English lesson for the day. Celia, who happened to be in the same hour as she, slid a note over to her desk. Felicia glanced up at Mrs. Harmon before opening the note. That woman had the eyes of an eagle. She could spot someone either passing a note or reading one a mile away! She claimed to be the queen of note passers, but Felicia felt that she and Celia had surpassed Mrs. Harmon's ability. They had been passing notes all year through and are yet to be caught. And now that it was spring, she doubted they would ever get caught.

As Mrs. Harmon droned on about the importance that Shakespeare had in literature, Felicia read Celia's note.

hey chick !!! TGIF heeh .... I don't think I could take 1 more of this old bat if I had 2 ... as if we r going 2 use this info ltr on when we r finally out of this jail they call high school. lol =I anyway.... I hear John is having a party 2morrow nite.... wanna go??? there is going 2 b this really HOT guy I want u 2 meet. His name is Jeff 23.... U will totally like him!!!

Felicia sighed. Celia was also more into parties than she was. But, she didn't want everyone to think of her as a prude, so she went along with her friend whenever there was a party, and she wrote back,

hey!!! sure i would luv 2 go!!!! I'll tell my parents I'm staying w/u so we can stay out as 18 as we want... ur parents are sooo much kooler than mine... when it comes 2 curfews,. okay gunna go....... da old bat is starting 2 watch me o.o catch u after skool =]:

Felicia slid the note back to Celia just as Mrs. Harmon turned around to ask the class a question. Felicia turned her mind back to the task at hand, Shakespeare, and impatiently waited for this long day to end. Even though she wasn't much of a partier, she was looking forward to Saturday just so she could get out of her house. Her siblings drove her crazy. *Soon,* she thought to herself, *soon I'll be able to move out and be on my own.*

Chapter 2

Felicia dropped her books on the bench in the hallway of her house. As she entered the kitchen to grab a snack, her older sister walked in.

"Mom is going to jump all over you if you leave your books in the hallway," Allison pointedly told her. "You know the rules, all of our stuff has to go to our rooms the minute we get home."

Felicia rolled her eyes at Allison. Allison was always trying to tell her what to do. Just because Allison was eighteen months older than her didn't mean that she was Felicia's boss. However, Allison saw it differently. *Why couldn't Allison be like all the other kids she knew and go* away *for college?* Felicia thought to herself. Instead of voicing her thoughts, she just pointedly ignored Allison as she opened the refrigerator door and grabbed herself an apple. Munching noisily, she walked upstairs to her room. She could care less what the rules were in the house. She was sick of rules.

Felicia turned on her stereo and flopped on her bed to think about the day. While it had started crummy, it didn't turn out too bad. She thought she did OK in the geometry test. There weren't any proofs to complete, which made it a lot easier. Then her mind drifted to her conversation with Celia about the party Saturday night. It was going to be over at John's house, the best friend of Celia's latest boyfriend. His parents were going to be out of town so he was throwing a "small" party. Felicia snorted at the thought of "small." The last "small" party, Celia dragged her too had over fifty people there. She shuddered as she remembered the crowd. Not only was she not big on parties, she wasn't big on crowds either. Crowds ranked right up there with thunderstorms.

This was yet another secret that Felicia had; one that she dare not tell even her closest friends. As sure as someone found out, they would realize what a fraud she was. Felicia, the outgoing party person would quickly become Felicia, the big baby who needs to learn to grow up.

A car door slam brought her out of her reverie. "Crap, Mom's home," she muttered to herself. She braced herself for what was about to come.

"Felicia! Get down here and pick up your mess!" hollered her mom in a very aggravated tone.

Felicia got off her bed, tossed her apple core in the wastebasket by her desk, and tromped down the steps to the hallway where her mother was waiting for her.

"How many times do I have to tell you to take your school books, coat, and anything else you have to your room? I don't tell you things for my health, you know." Her mother continued to rant, "You are lucky that it was me that saw this and not your father! Then we *All* would be paying for your sloppiness!"

It was painfully obvious to Felicia that her mother had had a bad day at work. Usually she didn't go on longer than one sentence. However, Felicia was still feeling the effects from the storm last night and worrying about the upcoming party so she wasn't in a mood to be conciliatory toward her mom.

"They are only textbooks, Mom! Geez! You would think that I had strewn all of my clothes from the front door to the back door and hung my underwear in the trees outside!" shot back Felicia as she began to pick up her books.

"That's it, I've had enough of your disrespect. Go to your room until you think you can behave like a respectful person, one who understands how lucky she is to actually have a house to live in!" responded her mom.

Felicia sighed inwardly. Her mom hadn't deserved that outburst, but she just couldn't seem to stop herself. She quietly picked up her stuff and headed back upstairs. She would give her mom a few minutes to cool off before she headed back down to apologize. No matter how tired she was of rules, Felicia knew she had it pretty good when it came to her homelife. She had a lot of other friends whose parents either beat them on a daily basis for simple things like forgetting to put their toothbrush back in the toothbrush holder or just didn't care one way or another about what their child did.

About thirty minutes later, Felicia headed back downstairs to talk to her mom. She found her in the living room working on the laptop. "Hey, Mom," Felicia said. "I'm not bothering you, am I?" Her mom looked up from her work and shook her head. Felicia realized in that moment how tired her mom looked. It made her feel even worse for the outburst earlier. "Um, I wanted to tell you I was sorry for my behavior earlier. I know you and Dad work really hard for us, and you didn't deserve my disrespect." Felicia apologized.

"Thank you, Felicia," her mom responded. "I'm glad you realize that. Allison is almost done fixing dinner, so why don't you head into the kitchen and help her out."

The last thing Felicia wanted to do was help her sister, but since she had already given her mom grief tonight, she went without complaint. She meandered into the beige and green kitchen. She always loved the look of their kitchen, the windows by the table faced west so there were always beautiful sunsets to watch while eating dinner. Her dad hated the green color, saying that it reminded him of the drab green he used to wear in the Army. He spent twenty years in the Army, and it always came through when he was ordering Felicia and her sister and brother around.

"Hey, Al. Mom wanted me to come in here and help get dinner on the table," Felicia informed her sister. "By the way, where's Josh?" She had just realized that her ten-year old brother wasn't around. Actually, now that she thought of it, he wasn't there at the door when she came home ready to bug her. She actually liked her little brother, but there was no way she was going to tell him that!

"Huh? Oh, Josh is over at Aaron's house," explained Allison. "From what Mom says he is eating dinner tonight over there, again." Josh practically lived at Aaron's house. He was lucky; his best friend lived two houses down. Felicia's best friend, actually all of her friends, lived across town. It sucked to live so far away from all of her friends. "Here, put these on the table," Allison told her, pulling Felicia out of her thoughts. As Felicia got the table ready for dinner she chatted with Allison about her classes she had that day. Just thinking about the day she could go to college gave her butterflies in her stomach, yet she couldn't wait. She envied Allison for only having two classes today.

About fifteen minutes later, Felicia's dad came home from work, and they all sat down for dinner. Her parents had this thing about everyone sitting at the table to eat. Most nights it didn't bug her. It was kind of nice to eat as a family. But there were nights when she would much rather eat dinner up in her room and listen to music. Tonight was one of those nights.

"So, how was your day?" asked her dad to no one in particular.

"It was busy, and I still have several hours of work to do," her mom provided. Her mom was some bigwig for an international company. Since she could do most of her work through webcams, she rarely had to travel overseas anymore. But she still put in sixty hours or more a week. There were many days when Felicia felt like she didn't even have a mom in the house.

"Mom, you work too much," Allison voiced Felicia's thoughts. Now that she was in college she thought she knew everything and didn't hesitate to let people know that. "I personally," she went on, not giving her mother a chance to reply, "had a fabulous day! We began studying Eleanor Roosevelt in my history class. She was fascinating!" Felicia quickly tuned her sister out. Like she really cared about Eleanor Roosevelt and the impact she had in politics.

The minute her sister paused in her newfound knowledge, Felicia jumped in. "I think I passed my geometry test today. Oh, and Celia is having a sleepover tomorrow night. Can I go?"

"As long as your chores are done before you leave, I don't see why you can't," her father replied. Felicia held her breath as she looked at her mom. She hoped that today's outburst didn't ruin her chances of going. Even though her dad already gave his permission, if her mom said no, then her dad would back her up. Her mom stopped eating and looked at Felicia. "Well, I guess as long as you get your normal chores done and clean the bathroom, you can go."

Felicia knew that the bathroom duty was because of the outburst, but she wasn't going to complain. The fact that her mom didn't tell her dad about the outburst right then meant that she wasn't going to say anything at all. Felicia grinned at her mom and dad.

"Thanks! I'm done eating, may I be excused? I'm dying to call Celia and tell her I can stay the night."

With her parents' nods, Felicia got up from the table and hurried upstairs to her room. As she shut the door and turned on the stereo, she grabbed her cell phone and called Celia. As soon as she answered, Felicia shouted in the phone, "I can go tomorrow!" She pulled the phone away from her ear as Celia squealed.

"That is so cool! You didn't tell your parents about the party, did you?"

"Are you kidding? I wouldn't be allowed out of the house if they knew about that."

"I didn't think you would tell them, but I just had to ask. So, what time are you coming over? The party starts at 8:00., and we have to have time to get ready!" Celia rambled on.

"I can come over as soon as I get done with my chores. I have an added chore because I blew up at my mom," Felicia said.

"Eww, that sucks. I swear you are the only person I know who has chores! I feel for you."

"Gee, thanks," Felicia responded sarcastically. She didn't need to be reminded that her parents lived in the dark ages. According to them, chores built character and respect. She guessed that it probably did, but she wouldn't let her friends know she thought that.

"OK, I gotta go. Mom is yelling for me to babysit my little brother. Text me later if you can. If not, I'll see you tomorrow!" Celia told her.

"Sure, sounds like a plan." As Felicia hung up the phone, she had the strangest feeling that tomorrow night was going to change her life. *What a ridiculous thought.* Felicia told herself. *However, it would be nice to meet the man of my dreams there. Summer is getting closer, and it would be great to start it with a boyfriend who could come by and take me places.* Not having a car really limited her on what she could do, and having a boyfriend with a car would be a major plus. She continued to daydream about the guy Celia and Cole wanted to introduce her to. Soon, Felicia drifted off to sleep with thoughts of the upcoming party.

Chapter 3

Felicia woke up on Saturday feeling much better. Her dreams were peaceful, which helped calm her nerves about the upcoming party that night. With that thought, she climbed out of bed to get ready for what her mom called "Chore Day." She personally called it "Hell Day" because she hated doing chores. As she made her bed, she created a mental list of what had to be done before she could escape to Celia's.

She had sent a text to Celia before she went to bed the night before to make arrangements for Celia to pick her up. It was decided between the two of them that she would come around noon. That gave Felicia four hours to get her room, the bathroom, and kitchen cleaned. Her room was going to be easy since the "mess" was just clothes all over the floor. Obviously, her parents didn't like her organizational skills when it came to her clothes. While she kept telling them that she knew where every piece of clothing was in all that mess, they still wanted everything in closets and drawers. She decided to tackle all of her chores before getting dressed.

Felicia turned her stereo on to help her clean faster, turning it onto her favorite rock station. As she began cleaning, she heard a pounding on her door.

"Felicia! Turn that stereo down! You are going to wake the whole neighborhood with that racket!" her father shouted through the door.

Felicia calmly walked to the door and opened it to find her dad standing on the other side. Noticing the redness in his face, she could tell that now was not the time to come back with a smart comment about how there was no earthly way the *whole* neighborhood would be woken up by her little stereo. At least, not if she wanted to go to Celia's for the night. So, she just looked up and said, "I'm sorry, Dad, I will turn it down." and turned around all the while rolling her eyes. It's not like she was committing a crime.

"Hmmmph!" was the answer that came from him as he shut her door.

Yep, it was time to put cleaning into high gear so she could get the hell out of there and find some freedom for twenty-four hours or more.

At about 12:30, Celia arrived to pick Felicia up. She came inside the house without even knocking. *That was the best thing about best friends,* Felicia thought, *you could feel at home in each other's houses*. Celia took one look at Felicia who was just finishing up the dishes, the last chore on her list, and just stared.

"What are you wearing?" asked Celia, more out of confusion than curiosity.

Felicia glanced down and laughed. She forgot that she still had her pajamas on. Last night she decided she wanted to wear one of her dad's brown T-shirts, the ones that were 100 percent cotton and the softest one could ever imagine, and a pair of purple-checkered boxers. She must look totally ridiculous to anyone walking in off the street.

"What? You don't like my outfit?" Felicia asked.

"You aren't seriously wearing that, are you?" Celia was still gaping at her.

"Sure I am," teased Felicia. Celia was such an easy target when it came to teasing.

"Over my dead body! I absolutely refuse to let my best friend go outside in an outfit that looks like something someone just puked up!" exclaimed Celia.

This made Felicia laugh harder. "Get real, Celia! Do you actually think I would go anywhere looking like this?"

"Well, there are times I do wonder about you," laughed Celia.

"I'm still in my pajamas. I didn't want to change until I was done cleaning," explained Felicia. "But, now that I'm done," she said as she started the dish washer, "I will run upstairs and change. I will shower at your house before we go to the party."

"Well, hurry up. I don't want to stay here too long. Your parents may think of something else for you to do before you leave," Celia said as she started shoving Felicia in the direction of her bedroom.

Once they got to the room they discussed what each was going to wear to the party. They both agreed upon jeans, some cute flats that Felicia bought the other day, and a purple tank to layer with a white tank. Purple always looked good on Felicia, and it made her feel empowered. She was going to need all the good feelings, she could muster up for this party. According to Celia the party had grown, just as Felicia figured it would.

With clothes figured out, and her overnight bag packed, Felicia went to seek out her parents. She found them in the now-clean kitchen eating lunch. *It never fails,* Felicia lamented, *I clean one area and the rest of the family dirties it. So, what is the point of cleaning in the first place??* She walked in and let them know that she was leaving with Celia.

"OK, honey," said her mom. "Be sure to let Celia's parents know if you girls go anywhere tonight. I need to know where you are, in case there is an emergency."

Felicia rolled her eyes. Her mom was way overprotective, and it drove her crazy. Yet one more thing she won't miss when she leaves for college. "I sure will," responded Felicia, not letting out her true feelings.

Her dad had to get his two cents in as well—it never failed, and it was always the same speech. Felicia could recite it with him. She did that once, but that just got her into trouble and she learned to keep her mouth shut. "Don't go running with any boy. Be sure to follow the Ryan's rules and curfews. I don't want to hear from Captain Leathers that you were out at one of the parties that the police or sheriff departments bust."

Felicia almost made the mistake of groaning out loud. She hated that her dad knew just about every police officer and deputy in the city and county. She couldn't do anything without someone finding out and it eventually getting back to her dad. Hell, she couldn't walk through Walmart without someone saying, "Hey, aren't you Carl and Mary Morgan's kid?" And she would always respond as politely as possible, "Yes, I am," which would always lead that person to the next inevitable comment, "You know, you look just like your mother." How she hated that. She was her own self, with her own personality. Why couldn't anyone ever look past that? But, she was always polite, because if she wasn't, it would get back to her parents, and then she would be grounded for life for being disrespectful.

"Don't worry, Dad," Felicia responded, "I always follow the rules. You know that." Felicia hoped she wouldn't go to hell for that small lie.

"We know, sweetie," her mom replied, stepping into her dad's long speech. "I'm sure you will be good and have a wonderful time. Be home by tomorrow afternoon. Love you." Her mom came over and gave her a hug. Felicia quickly hugged her back and looked over at Celia. They both shared the look that said, "Let's get the hell out of here!"

Celia grabbed Felicia's bag as she grabbed her purse. As they walked toward Celia's car, which Felicia absolutely was envious over, she noted to her friend, "I thought we were never going to get out of there! Once my dad starts on his speeches, he can go on forever! Thank God my mom stepped in, otherwise we would still be standing there. And by the way, have I told you that I totally love your car? Not just because you have one and I don't, I really like it." Felicia slid into the passenger seat of Celia's 1966 Mustang convertible. It was a gorgeous night-mist blue with a cream interior. Celia was lucky to have an older brother who was into restoring old cars. It was how she was able to get this one.

Celia chuckled, "Yeah, I think you've mentioned liking my car a time or two. When are you going to get one of your own?"

"God, I wish it was today! My parents have this thing about us not having a car until we are eighteen. And even then it will probably be some clunker. But, at least it will be *my* clunker!" Felicia sat quiet for a moment and then asked, "So, what time are we going to the party?"

"Oh, I told Cole we would meet him over at John's around 8 or 9. You know no one will actually be there until 9:00, anyway. And, he is bringing Jeff along so you can meet him! I think you are going to totally love him!" gushed Celia.

"So what does he look like? And how do you know I will like him? Does he like the same stuff as me?" asked Felicia. "You've just barely mentioned him but yet you keep saying how I'm going to like him."

"Well," Celia paused to collect her thoughts. "I've only met him once so I don't remember much about his likes and dislikes, but I can tell you what he looks like." He is about Cole's height, 5'11", and has sandy blonde hair with these gorgeous blue eyes. You will love his eyes! He dresses nice, I do remember that. Oh, and he isn't from around here but from a town south of here. He is up here visiting family for the summer. His school is already out."

"They are already out??" Felicia asked staring at Celia. "They are so lucky! We still have three weeks to go!"

"I know our school district sucks. We start early and end late. How screwed up is that?" Celia complained. This was a common complaint of all Rosewood's students.

"Well, Jeff sounds kinda cute. I guess I'm looking forward to meeting him. But if I totally hate him, we are leaving the party immediately!"

"What?!" exclaimed Celia.

"I'm serious, Celia. I don't want to hang around a jerk all night." Felicia explained.

"OK, fine. But only if he is a total jerk." Felicia was surprised that Celia complied so quickly. She wondered if Celia had something up her sleeve. Either that or she was so positive that Felicia would like Jeff that she had nothing to worry about. Felicia hoped it was the latter.

They arrived at the Ryan home and went upstairs to start getting ready for the party. They had several hours, but they would need every minute available. They both had to shower, fix their hair and makeup, and lots of gossiping to do before hand.

As they entered Celia's room, which was covered in posters of all of her favorite rock bands, they sat on the bed and began to chat. "OMG, Felicia, did you hear what Susie Dorscher did Friday in biology class??" started Celia.

"Um, I don't think so. But, with Susie there is no telling." Felicia sat back on Celia's bed, got comfortable, and waited for Celia to start the tale.

"Well, you know they are dissecting frogs this week. Susie took her scissors and . . ." as Celia told the story, Felicia's mind began to wander, thinking of the upcoming party. Jeff did sound kinda cute. She hoped he was as nice and cute as Celia made him out to be. *Hmmm, a guy from out of town who would not know my parents. What a great idea. I would have more freedom talking to a person like that.* As Felicia continued to think about Jeff, she made sure she put an "um hm" and "no way" in the proper place as Celia went on with the story. Tonight was starting to look up. She was beginning to look forward to this party.

Chapter 4

The girls spent about two hours on their hair and makeup while jamming to Celia's latest CD purchase and munching on the dinner they scrounged up. The Ryan's didn't hold the dinner traditions that the Morgan's did. They had found leftover pizza in the fridge, threw a few pieces in the microwave and headed back up the Celia's room. Yet another rule Felicia had to follow that Celia didn't—no food in the room. Felicia envied the lack of rules Celia had in her house.

Using a straightener on Felicia's hair, Celia worked to turn all of her hated curls into a gorgeous straight hair look. "I don't know why you hate your curls so much," Celia commented, "I would love to have curls like yours."

"Curls are fine if they are 'in', but they aren't. Plus, on humid days those cute curls turn into a messy frizz." Felicia wrinkled her nose just thinking about it. "I would much rather have perfectly straight hairs like yours."

"Yeah, well there are days that my 'perfectly straight hair' as you put it drives me nuts. It won't hold a curl for more than an hour, and that is on a nonhumid day. And how many nonhumid days do we have here in Rosewood, Alabama? None," Celia responded with disgust.

"If only we could switch hair for a day!" Felicia giggled at the image that brought. She had never pictured herself with anything but red hair. She might like going blonde. Maybe more guys would notice her in a good way if she was a blonde. But, her parents would kill her if she dyed her hair.

"OK, I think that is the last of it," Celia commented as she sprayed half the can of hairspray on Felicia's hair. "And I think that should hold it for a while," she said with a grin.

"I would hope so! You obviously aren't concerned about the ozone layer after spraying half that can on my head!" laughed Felicia.

"No, not concerned, we will all die someday, whether it is because of global warming due to no ozone, or just walking across the street." This was one of the things that Felicia likes about Celia. She wasn't all caught up in all the supposedly good causes of the world. She looked at things matter-of-factly and went on with her life. The best part was that Celia didn't care if she pissed off a few people along the way by stating her opinion. *I would love to be able to do that,* Felicia thought.

Felicia laughed, not voicing her thoughts, instead saying, "I love your outlook on life, Celia!"

Celia grinned at her. "Righty-o my friend. Now that we look gorgeous, let's go knock some guys on the ground by our beauty!" She winked at Felicia as they headed toward the door.

"Bye, Mom! We'll be back later. We are going over to a friend's house for a bit and will probably go to a movie." Celia shouted into the living room.

"OK, dear. Have a good time," her mother answered absently as her attention was focused on the latest reality-TV show. Celia's mom was completely hooked on every reality show that came on.

Grinning at Felicia, Celia motioned with her head to go out to the car. Once in, Celia turned on the stereo up as loud as it would go and took off down the street toward John's house. It was a little before 9, by the time they pulled up to John's house; there was already a large amount of people there. John's parents were quite wealthy and had a large house with an in-ground swimming pool. They also took a lot of trips, so John took advantage of that and held many parties while they were gone.

As they walked up to the front door, they could hear the music playing, people laughing and talking loud. Instead of knocking, Felicia and Celia just walked in. The first person they saw was Cole. Celia ran up to him and gave him a big hug and kiss. Felicia rolled her eyes. By the way Celia acted, you would have thought that they hadn't seen each other for years.

"Hey!" said Cole. "I see you were able to get Felicia past the wardens in her house. That's cool. I think Jeff is over by the bar where the keg is." He pointed his head in the direction of the game room where John's parents had a wet bar.

Felicia stared at him. "I'm not going over there by myself! I'll look like a complete idiot."

Celia punched Cole in the arm, "Go get Jeff and bring him here to introduce to us, you dummy!"

"OK, whatever." Cole mumbled as he walked to the bar.

"Remember your promise," Felicia reminded Celia as Cole walked away.

"I remember, but don't worry, you're gonna love him."

Just then John came walking by. He stopped when he saw Celia and Felicia. "Awesome! The two best-looking chicks in school made it!" Felicia could tell John must have started drinking before the party even began because the word 'awesome' came out more like "awshum." John had a real issue with alcohol, and his parents didn't even know it.

"Hey, John. Great party you have going on," Celia told him. "Do you have the pool open?"

"Duh! What's a party without some swimming?"

"Cool, we will head out that way sometime tonight then."

"Well, I better go. Gotta get more beer for my peeps!" John waved as he sauntered, or well, more like stumbled off.

Felicia rolled her eyes and looked over at Celia who was doing the same. The girls started laughing as they read each other's thoughts.

"What's so funny?" asked Cole as he came walking back up to them with Jeff in tow.

"Oh, nothing. John was just by here. He's already had quite a bit to drink tonight hasn't he?" Celia pointed out.

"Yeah, but until his parents realize what is going on, that isn't going to change. And his parents are so into themselves, they will never notice what John is doing," Cole observed. Switching subjects, Cole looked at Jeff, "Hey Jeff, this is Felicia, the girl I told you about."

Jeff looked at Felicia and said, "She's cute!"

Felicia turned as red as her hair and said, "Thanks. It's nice to meet you."

"So, you want a drink?" asked Jeff.

"Sure, I would love one," Felicia answered even though she hated the taste of beer. She definitely didn't want him to think of her as some prissy girl. Jeff was pretty cute himself, and she already liked him. He had a great smile.

"Hey, grab one for me too," Celia told Jeff.

"Sure, no problem. Let's go, get the gals something to drink, Cole. We'll meet you girls out by the pool." Jeff said.

"Sounds good," Celia told them. She turned to look at Felicia and said, "Let's head out to the patio by the pool."

As soon as they were out of earshot of the guys, Felicia looked at Celia and said, "OMG! He is too cute! And his smile is to die for! I just hope his personality is just as good. You know how some guys are who are cute and know it. They are total jerks."

"Trust me, you'll like him. Cole wouldn't hang around any jerks," Celia assured her.

They reached the patio and grabbed some lounge chairs and pulled them together. The guys soon returned with their drinks and handed them to Celia and Felicia.

"So, Felicia, Cole tells me you are in the same class as him. Are you ready for school to be out?"

Felicia looked over at Jeff who was smiling at her. It was a good thing she was sitting because her knees went weak, and she felt butterflies in her stomach when she looked at that smile. "Um, yeah I am more than ready for school to be out. If only this was our senior year. That would make it all that much better," replied Felicia. She was quite proud of herself for being able to put more than two words together and sound halfway coherent. Usually, she became tongue-tied around cute guys.

"I hear ya on that one," agreed Jeff. "I'm ready for senior year to be here and over with as well." Cole and Celia chimed in their agreement as well.

"Here's to our upcoming senior year and then total freedom," Cole said raising his beer. The others raised their plastic cups, and they all "clanked" them together.

As the others drank, Felicia just sipped on her beer. She finally gathered the courage to ask Jeff, "So, where are you from? Celia said you weren't from around here."

"Yeah, I'm from St. Peters, which is about one hundred miles southeast of Rosewood. The town is about the same size as Rosewood. We have about twenty thousand people, but there is nothing much to do. So, I like to come up here to visit family during the summer. It lets me get away from my parents and younger sister," explained Jeff.

"That's cool that you have somewhere to go during the summer to get away. I really wish I had something like that. I have family out in California, but that is too far away, and my parents would never pay for a plane ticket for me to go there for a summer," Felicia told Jeff.

The four of them continued to talk, stopping every once in a while to watch the antics of John and the others that decided to go swimming. They were chicken-fighting with guys holding girls on their shoulders with the girls trying to knock each other off. Felicia and Celia cheered the girls on, while Cole and Jeff shouted instructions to the guys.

Around two in the morning the party started to wind down. Felicia and Celia decided it was time to leave. Cole and Jeff walked the girls to Celia's car. Jeff opened the car door for Felicia. She looked up in surprise. No guy had ever opened a car door for her! "Thanks, Jeff," Felicia said.

"No problem. Hey, I know you have school this week, but I would really like to see you again. Would you want to go out next weekend? Maybe catch a movie or something?" Jeff asked.

"I would love to. Here's my cell phone number. Just call me whenever," Felicia told him.

"Cool, thanks! I'll be talking to you later this week, then."

"Sounds great. Talk to you then." Felicia looked over at Celia. "Hey, Celia! Disengage yourself from Cole, so we can go!"

Celia stopped kissing Cole and turned to make a face at Felicia. She gave him one more quick kiss and then got into the car. "See you later, Cole. You too, Jeff!" Celia grinned at Jeff and waved.

As they drove back to Celia's house, Felicia looked out the window thinking of Jeff. Her thoughts were interrupted with Celia asking, "So? Did you like him? What did you think?"

Felicia wasn't sure she wanted to voice her thoughts just yet. She knew whatever she said to Celia would go straight to Cole, which would go straight to Jeff. "I don't know what I think just yet," Felicia told her friend. "He is definitely cute. We are supposed to go out next weekend. I'll let you know what I think after that."

Celia, knowing she wouldn't get Felicia to budge, shrugged her shoulders, "OK, have it your way." She turned up the radio and started singing as loud as she could.

Felicia turned back toward the window and her thoughts back to Jeff. So, how did she feel about him? She really wasn't sure. All she knew right now was that he made her knees weak and caused butterflies in her stomach when he smiled. *Could someone fall in love at first sight?* Felicia never thought anyone could fall in love that quick, but now she wasn't too sure.

Chapter 5

The school week dragged on for Felicia. She was completely ready for the weekend. She hadn't seen Celia all week except for in Mrs. Harmon's class. They didn't talk much then because Mrs. Harmon had finally split the two of them up, and now they were on opposite ends of the room from each other. She was dying to talk to Celia about Saturday night. They were not able to talk much after they got home from the party, and Felicia had to go home right after she woke up on Sunday. Then during the day on Sunday, she must have said something to tick off her mom; however, she had not a clue as to what that was. Either way, the result was she was grounded from her cell phone or any other device that would allow her to talk to Celia.

Felicia rolled her eyes at the memory. Whatever it was that set her mom off started a huge argument. Felicia remembered the words like it was yesterday.

"How dare you speak to me like that," her mother ground out.

"Like what, Mom? You are always blaming me for things I haven't done! And you claim I'm disrespectful to you, but yet you never tell me *how* I'm disrespectful," she responded.

"Don't play stupid with me. You know how you were disrespectful, and I've had it up to here with it!" her mom held her hand above her head. Her voice also kept going up a notch as she yelled.

"But, Mom, I'm not playing . . ."

"That's it! No more talking back!" her mom interrupted her. "Hand over your cell phone right now. You have lost all cell phone privileges until this weekend. You will only gain back those privileges if you can speak to me in a respectful manner."

Felicia had handed over her cell phone still confused as to what she did. She sighed as she walked slowly to lunch. It had been a long week since she couldn't talk to Celia. She had no idea if Jeff had tried to call her. What if he had tried to call or text and she didn't answer? Would he think that she didn't want to go out this weekend? Would he think she was some snob and decide to blow her off? She hoped not. She had really enjoyed her talk with him Saturday night at the party. She wanted to see him again, badly.

As Felicia grabbed her food, she headed outside to the green and yellow picnic tables. She thought the tables were ugly, painted in the school colors, but at least it allowed them to eat someplace else besides inside the school building. She glanced around and found Celia quickly by her bright yellow hair with a cute pink hat atop. Celia always wore something unusual. Felicia envied her; she wished she had that devil-may-care attitude that Celia had. Celia could care less what others thought about her.

"Hey, Celia!" Felicia hollered.

Celia turned around and waved enthusiastically. "Hey, Felicia! Come on over! I've been dying to talk to you!"

"Where have you been this week? I've only seen you in English class but not at lunch." Felicia noted.

Celia rolled her eyes. "Oh, dumb old Mr. Felzworth in science gave me lunch detention for three days! I had to eat lunch with him in his classroom. It was disgusting! That man doesn't know how to eat properly. I swear half the food he ate landed on his tie. And the worst part is he would chew with his mouth open! Ugh! I practically lost my appetite while I was in there. All I could hear was his chomping," Celia ended with a big demonstration of what she meant. This sent Felicia into a fit of giggles.

"Oh, I'm sorry, Celia! I don't mean to laugh, but the look on your face was too funny! You never have gotten along with Mr. Felzworth."

"I can't wait for this year to be over, and then I will be done with that man! No more science for me!" Celia exclaimed.

"Well, we just have this week and then finals week and then we are finished! It can't come too soon for me," said Felicia.

"So, I've been dying to ask you about last Saturday night!" Celia said, switching subjects. "Did you like him?"

"Like who?" Felicia asked, knowing it would drive Celia nuts.

"'Like who?' she calmly asks. You *know* who!! Jeff! What did you think about him? Are you guys going out again? What's going on?" Celia shot all the questions at her like a gun.

"Well, I haven't talked to him since Saturday, but . . ."

"What? You haven't talked to him since Saturday? Why not?" Celia demanded.

"Because, if you would stop to think for just a second, you would remember that I have no cell phone right now! Duh!" responded Felicia. "Now will you let me continue?"

"Oh, yeah, sorry I forgot about that whole cell phone incident. Go on with your story. I promise not to interrupt." Celia tried to look as contrite as possible, which was no easy feat for her.

Felicia grinned. "Well, as for Saturday night I had a great time talking to him. We had a lot in common, and he was totally hot like you said. He did tell me when we were at your car that he wanted to see me again. So we are supposed to go out this coming weekend. But, since I haven't had my phone, I don't know if he still wants to go out!" Felicia expressed her concern about Jeff not liking her.

"I'll call Cole tonight and have him give Jeff a call and explain the whole phone situation. I'll have him give Jeff your home number so he can call you tonight," offered Celia. "And as for not liking you, he would be totally stupid if he didn't like you! What's not to like?" That was what Felicia loved about Celia, she was always so positive and helped her feel good about herself. Celia was the only person who knew how terribly shy Felicia really was. That was the one and only secret that she ever told anyone. And she knew she could trust Celia to keep that secret. In fact, Celia worked hard to bring Felicia out of the shell that she put around herself sometimes.

Thanks, Celia. I appreciate this. I owe you one." Felicia gave her friend a hug just as the bell rang for the students to report to the next hour. Felicia got up and headed to class feeling a little better knowing that Jeff would find out what was really going on and that she just wasn't ignoring any phone calls or text messages.

~*~*~*~*~*~*~*~*~*~*~

That evening as the Morgans were sitting around the dinner table, the phone rang. Felicia's dad stood up to answer it. As a rule, there were no phone calls during dinnertime. Having family time around the dinner table was considered sacred in her parents' eyes. Personally, Felicia would rather just take her food to her room, close her door, and eat while listening to music. But, she endured the routine. She enjoyed the privileges that obeying the rules gave her. And if Jeff still wanted to go out this weekend, she didn't want to be grounded.

Her dad came back to the table and sat down. He looked at Felicia and told her, "That phone call was for you. It was a guy named Jeff Saunders. I told him you were eating and that this family would not take phone calls between the times of 6 p.m. and 7 p.m."

Felicia looked stunned. "You seriously didn't tell him that, did you, Dad?"

"Yes, young lady, I did. Now, explain to me who this young man is."

Felicia had to think quick. She couldn't possibly tell her parents that she met him at a party and had a few beers with him. Talk about getting into trouble that would land her in purgatory for life! She smiled as she thought of the perfect explanation, "Well, I met him at the movies last Saturday night. When I stayed the night with Celia, her parents let us go to the early show. Cole, Celia's boyfriend you know, was there with his friend Jeff. The guys decided to watch the same movie as us. So, that is how I met him."

"Hmm, is he from around here? I don't recognize that last name," observed her dad.

"No, he is visiting relatives for the summer. He is originally from St. Peters."

Felicia's dad looked over at her mom. After a moment he asked, "Do you know who his relatives are?"

"I really didn't think to ask him, Dad. If he calls back, I can if you need me to," offered Felicia.

"Not necessary, and yes, he is supposed to call back. I told him to call you back after 7," he informed her.

Felicia let out a breath one didn't even realize she was holding until her dad said that Jeff would be calling back. This must mean the groundment was lifted for at least the home phone, and she wasn't about to remind them of being grounded. "Thanks, Dad," Felicia smiled up at her dad. *He isn't that bad of a dad, I guess.* Felicia thought to herself. *He just looks out for his family and values at family time. That's why he is so strict sometimes.* She realized her dad was talking to her mom again and heard Jeff's name.

"I'll call Cy tomorrow and see if he can't find out information about the Saunders family in St. Peters," he said to her mom. Cy was her dad's best friend and the captain of the police force in town. His real name wasn't Cy, it was Cyrus. Everyone called him Cy since he hated the name Cyrus.

Felicia inwardly sighed. She should be used to this, her dad having Captain Leathers looking up the guys she dates. But no matter how many times he does it, it still bothers her. But, it was not worth arguing over. Arguing would just get her in trouble again.

As dinner ended, Felicia helped Josh clear the table and take the dishes into the kitchen. In the midst of helping, the phone rang. Felicia ran to the phone yelling, "I got it!" She grabbed the phone before her mom or dad could pick up. Or even worse, her older sister.

"Hello?" Felicia answered, slightly breathless from running to the phone.

"May I please speak to Felicia?" asked this deep voice. Felicia recognized it in a second. It could only belong to one person, Jeff.

"This is Felicia," she responded, not wanting him to know that she recognized his voice. She didn't want him to think she had been mooning over him for the past five days.

"Hey, Felicia, this is Jeff."

"Hey, Jeff! Did Cole get a hold of you?" asked Felicia.

"Yeah, he called me earlier. Man, was I glad to hear that I hadn't heard back from you because you lost your cell phone. I thought you were just ignoring my messages," said Jeff.

"No, not ignoring you. It was taken away on Sunday. I get it back tomorrow night," explained Felicia.

"So, um, are you still interested in going out this weekend?" Jeff asked.

"Yeah, sure, I would love to go out," she replied, hoping she didn't sound too eager or desperate.

"Cool, how about tomorrow night?"

"Um, let me make sure if that is OK with my parents. They have this thing about asking before doing. They are really big into rules," Felicia told him.

"Yeah, not a prob. I'll hold, you go ask."

"K, I'll be right back." Felicia ran into the other room where her parents sat putting together a puzzle. Sometimes she thought her parents must be the most boring parents in the whole school! She quickly asked her parents about going out tomorrow night, got the nods of their heads, and dashed back to the phone. *Why on earth her parents refused to buy a cordless is beyond me.* Felicia thought to herself. *I guess I should just be happy if they let us have cell phones.*

She reached the phone, "You still there?"

"Yup, still here. I wouldn't go anywhere with you on the other line," he told her.

Once again Felicia felt the butterflies in her stomach. "Well, they said I could go on one condition. You have to come here to pick me up so they can meet you," Felicia told him. She crossed her fingers hoping that that wouldn't turn him off. "They are sorta old fashioned," she explained.

"No, that's cool. I admire that in parents. I would do the same if I had a daughter as pretty as you," Jeff said.

Felicia blushed and was glad, no one was around to see her bright red face. "Great! Then I'll see you tomorrow night. What time?"

"How about around 7:00?"

"Sounds perfect," Felicia told him. She quickly gave him directions and then they hung up. *Well, it wasn't the longest of conversations I've had with people, but at least I'm going out tomorrow night! And with a really cute guy!* Felicia did a little skip and jump and headed up to her room smiling what must have been the most ridiculous smile on anyone's face. She was glad that she didn't run into Josh or Allison right then. She didn't want to explain herself, or be teased. Tomorrow night couldn't come fast enough for Felicia.

Chapter 6

Finally, it is here! Felicia thought to herself. She was under strict orders from Celia to give her a detailed account of her date with Jeff tonight. Felicia glanced at her clock and saw that it was almost 7. She checked her makeup and hair once more before leaving her room and headed downstairs to wait.

As she walked into the living room, she saw her mom and dad sitting and talking. The moment they saw her they stopped, and she knew right then they were talking about her. She was afraid they were going to tell her they had changed their minds that she couldn't go out with Jeff that night. *Oh please, Lord, don't let them take away the one night I've been looking forward to all week!*

"Hey, Sweetheart," her mom said. "Your dad and I were just talking about you." She smiled warmly over at Felicia. Just by that smile, Felicia knew that they weren't going to tell her she couldn't go tonight. She inwardly sighed with relief.

"Oh yeah? What about?" Felicia asked.

"About this guy you are going out with tonight."

Felicia froze. Maybe she was wrong. Maybe they were going to tell her she couldn't go. She started thinking about sneaking out if they did this to her. She had never done anything like that before, but she *really* wanted to go out with Jeff. He seemed so nice, unlike all the other jerks at her school.

"What about Jeff?" Felicia asked cautiously.

"Well, your dad has talked to Cy who had a nice visit with some friends he has down in St. Peters. It seems that

your Jeff comes from a very nice family," her mom told her
with a smile on her face.

"So, I can still go out tonight?"

"Most definitely. However," her mom paused.

Great, thought Felicia, *they are going to put conditions
on my date. Just what I freakin' need.*

"We would like to meet this young man and visit with
him for a minute before you guys go out tonight," her mom
finished.

"And," her dad interjected, "I've promised your mother
that I would not ask any embarrassing questions, or to
embarrass you in anyway."

"Cool," Felicia smiled with relief. She could live with this
request. "He was already planning on coming in and meeting
you both anyway," she informed them. She was suddenly
very glad she had thought ahead on the possible conditions
her parents might throw at her at the last minute.

About that time the doorbell rang. Her dad went to answer
the door and Felicia could hear Jeff's deep voice asking for
her. Just the sound of his voice made her knees weak.

"So, what do you kids plan on doing tonight?" her dad
was asking Jeff as they walked into the living room.

"Well, sir," Jeff replied, "I hope we can catch the latest
movie at the theaters and go for sodas afterward, if that
meets your approval."

Felicia smiled. He was so polite! Her parents would eat
that up! She almost laughed at the thought of how he was
schmoozing up to her parents. But, she controlled herself. It
would make leaving so much easier if they believed he was
this polite. He was polite to her as well, but not like this.
This was totally his "talking to parents" face.

"That sounds fine with us. So, Felicia tells us you are
from St. Peters," her dad began the inquisition, as Felicia
liked to call it.

"Yes, sir," Jeff responded with a smile.

"A friend of ours has some friends down there. Do you
know the Russell family?" he asked.

Jeff nodded his head, "I sure do. My parents are friends
with the Russell's. They are a nice family."

"Well, they had nice things to say about your family as well." Her dad was making sure that Jeff realized that he had checked up on the Saunders family.

"Thank you, sir," Jeff said.

"Well, you kids have a great time tonight. Have her back by 11:00 p.m.," her dad instructed Jeff.

"Not a problem, sir," Jeff said with a smile.

Felicia got up from her chair and walked with Jeff to the front door. "Bye, Mom! Bye, Dad!" she hollered back to the living room and then quickly took Jeff to and out the front door.

Jeff started laughing the minute they were outside. He turned and looked at Felicia with a warm light in his eyes. "You look hot tonight," he told her.

Felicia blushed in bright red again. How she hated how easily she blushed! "Thanks, Jeff."

He grabbed her hand and led her to his truck. "So, are they always like that? I mean, does your dad always check into the guys you are going out with?"

Felicia rolled her eyes as she got in the truck, noticing how he opened the door for her. "Unfortunately, yes, they are always like this. I hate it! Talk about feeling smothered by overprotective parents!"

"Well, I'm really glad my parents aren't like that! It would drive me nuts," Jeff told her.

"So, where are we really going?" asked Felicia.

"I was serious about the movie thing, if you are interested in doing that."

"Sure, sounds great!"

They headed over to the local theater where they saw many of Felicia's friends from high school. Jeff bought her some popcorn with extra butter, just the way she liked it, and a Coke to drink. They decided to share a large soda and popcorn since they could get refills. He held her hand as they went in to find seats. The warmth of his hand made her feel warm inside. *This must be love!* Felicia thought. *I have never felt like this with any other guy!*

When they were settled in their seats, Jeff put his arm around her. All through the movie, she kept expecting him to make a move on her. Other guys she had dated always tried to make a move on the first date. She was pleasantly surprised when the movie was over and not once did he try anything more than to hold her hand or put his arm around her shoulders.

After the movie, they went out for sodas at the local pizza joint. As they walked in, they saw Cole and Celia sitting in a booth. Celia saw them at the same time and was waving frantically. Felicia started to laugh. Celia looked like a bird trying to take off with only one wing.

"Hey guys!" Celia practically shouted, smiling really big. "Where have you been?"

"We went to see a movie," Felicia explained as they slid into the booth.

"And," interjected Jeff, "if we want to keep your parents happy, we only have thirty more minutes before you have to be home."

Felicia made a face at him. "I hate curfews! But, I guess you're right. If I don't get home on time, it will destroy my going out anytime soon."

"Well, we definitely don't want that to happen," Jeff told her. "I hope to go out many more times this summer." He gave her a smile that warmed her heart and once again making her knees weak. She smiled shyly back.

"OK, we'll see you guys later, then," Celia was saying bringing Felicia out of the trance that Jeff seems to bring on when he smiles.

"Yeah, see you later," Felicia said waving bye to them.

"See ya, man," Jeff said to Cole, and he led Felicia outside by the hand.

By the time Jeff drove Felicia home, she decided that she definitely liked his smiles and holding hands. It made her feel as if she was free and cherished.

Jeff parked in front of her house, got out, and opened the car door for her. They slowly walked to her front door, where the light glared like a beacon. It was one of the many safety measures, her dad always seemed to be putting in place. They stopped at the door, and Felicia turned to Jeff.

"I had a great time tonight, Jeff. Thanks for asking me out."

"Me too, Felicia. And I was serious about what I said back at the restaurant. I would like to go out again." Jeff leaned forward and whispered, "I think you are pretty special."

Felicia looked up into his eyes and got butterflies in her stomach. *He's going to kiss me!* Felicia thought to herself. She didn't know what to expect, and was pleasantly surprised when he gave her a soft kiss on the lips. Nothing demanding, nothing forceful. It was a small, respectful, yet very delicious kiss.

Jeff backed away and smiled saying goodnight. He headed to his car. Felicia stood there staring after him, smiling to herself. *This,* she thought, *is a guy I can trust. I think I might be in love!* And slowly she turned and went inside.

Chapter 7

Summer came with a vengeance. It became hot and miserable, even for Alabama, very quickly. Jeff and Felicia went out more and more often. Felicia's parents loved Jeff, so they didn't care if and when she went out with him. Felicia loved the newfound freedom.

One summer night, as they were cruising town, they ran into Celia. Cole was nowhere to be found, so they invited her to join them in cruising. The three teens crammed in the front seat of Jeff's little black S-10. He had customized his truck by taking out the bucket seats and putting in a bench seat, which made it a little easier to fit three people in the front.

As they were driving down the main strip, Jeff turned to Felicia and said, "Grab the wheel."

She looked at him with confusion in her eyes. "What?"

"I said, grab the wheel."

Felicia laughed, "OK, but I don't understand why you want me to take the wheel while you are driving."

"Because," Jeff grinned wickedly, "I am going to crawl out my window, go across the back of the truck, and then come in the passenger window."

Felicia just stared at him. "You are not!" She couldn't believe what she was hearing. They could get caught by the cops or worse, crash into someone.

"Sure I am. Trust me, I've done it before," Jeff told her.

Celia sat over on her side of the truck laughing. "Oh my God, that is hilarious! Take the wheel, Felicia! Don't be such a loser!"

Not wanting to look like she was afraid of anything and ruin her chance with a great boyfriend, Felicia took the wheel as Jeff started to crawl out the window. Felicia's palms started to sweat. *Oh My God! I can't even freaking believe I'm doing this! If we wreck, my parents will kill me, and I will never be allowed out again! That is if we live through this in the first place!* Felicia started to scoot over to Jeff's spot. As she took over the wheel completely, the truck swerved toward the oncoming traffic. Celia shrieked, and Jeff hollered at her as he was crawling across the back, "Keep the damn wheel straight, and we won't crash!"

At the same time Celia was yelling, "Don't swerve! Keep the wheel straight!"

Felicia got the truck under control and back into her lane just as the other car whizzed by. She was shaking and looked over at Celia, who was now sitting in the middle. Celia was laughing uncontrollably. "I don't think that was very funny," Felicia hissed at her.

"Oh, come on! You really need to loosen up, Felicia!"

Just then, Jeff crawled through the passenger window. "What a rush!" he exclaimed. "Wasn't that a blast?" He was laughing with Celia.

Felicia forced out a chuckle, "Yeah, I totally loved that! We gotta do it again!"

"We are, it's your turn," Jeff told her.

Felicia looked over at him like he had just sprouted two horns from his head. "You can't be serious!"

"Sure I am. It's easy, don't worry," he assured her.

"No, you don't understand," Felicia started to feel panicky. "I am an absolute klutz! I would end up falling off the truck."

Celia started laughing again. "Well, she does have a point. I have never met someone as klutzy as Felicia. She even trips herself sometimes!" Jeff started laughing with Celia.

Felicia looked over at the two of them, not seeing the humor in her inability to stay upright all the time. Unfortunately, her clumsiness was one aspect of herself that she couldn't hide from people.

"OK," Jeff said, still laughing, "I won't make you do that this time. I would hate to see you fall or something." He gave her one of those heart-stopping, knee-melting smiles.

Felicia smiled back, "Thanks."

Shortly after, they dropped Celia off at her car, and Jeff started to drive Felicia home. "Do you feel like going home yet?" he asked her when they were almost there.

"Not really. It feels like a prison sometimes."

"Wanna go hit the back roads for a while?"

"Sure, sounds like fun. But, I can't be gone too much longer."

"Not to worry," Jeff assured her, "I will have you home to the wardens before the sun rises." He gave her a wink to let her know he was joking. She smiled back and snuggled by his side.

They drove around for a bit before he pulled off onto one of the dark-side roads, one where very few cars passed by. "What are we doing here?" Felicia asked.

"I thought this would be a good spot for us to just sit and snuggle for a while," he whispered leaning toward her.

As he kissed her, Felicia felt the butterflies in her stomach again. She could definitely get used to his kisses. They sat there for a while kissing when she felt Jeff's hand move to her chest. Felicia wasn't sure about the direction he was headed. She broke from the kiss just as a car passed by.

"Why did you stop?" he asked a little breathlessly.

"Um, I." Felicia didn't know what to say. She didn't want him to think she was a prude but she wasn't really ready to go any farther than they already had. "The headlights of the car surprised me." She was proud of herself for thinking quickly on her feet, something she rarely can do. Felicia looked at the clock on the dash of his truck. "You probably ought to get me home."

Jeff looked at the time and sighed. "Yeah, I guess you're right."

Felicia inwardly sighed with relief. He drove her home in silence, with just the music from the radio filling the cab of the truck. Felicia felt uncomfortable with what happened but didn't know how to explain herself to Jeff.

Jeff pulled up to her house and parked on the street. He turned to Felicia, "So are we still on for the movies Friday?"

Felicia smiled. She didn't realize how much she was worried that he would break up with her until that moment. "Yeah, sure. I would love to still go."

"Great, I'll pick you up around 7:00 tomorrow night then," he grinned that devastating smile and gave her a quick kiss. Felicia got out of his truck and walked up to her house, feeling happy that she had a boyfriend who seemed to respect her. Life couldn't get better than this.

Chapter 8

Felicia's summer was flying by. She spent most days and nights with Jeff. They went to the movies a lot and hit the local teen dance club almost every night it was open. Jeff never tried anything more than a kiss since the night in his truck, and Felicia was silently grateful for that.

One afternoon in early August, Felicia invited Jeff over to listen to some music. Her parents and Josh were at the store getting school supplies. She had no idea where Allison was, and really didn't care. She knew her time was growing short with Jeff. He would be leaving that weekend for home, and school would start back up in another week.

Felicia was going into the kitchen to get something to drink when she heard a knock on the door. She smiled as she went to open it.

"Hey, Jeff. I'm really glad you were able to come over," she said smiling at him.

"I'm really glad you invited me. You look great today," he said as his eyes traveled from her face down to her feet.

Felicia blushed. She still wasn't used to compliments like this. She had chosen her outfit with care that day, hoping to impress Jeff. She had on her favorite jean skirt that came to just above her knees. She decided to layer her tank tops, a white one with her favorite yellow one over it. She loved yellow and how it looked on her. It made her feel beautiful, and the color always reminded her of sunny days. She was glad her efforts paid off and that Jeff liked how she looked.

"Um, thanks," she told him, still blushing. "Come on inside. I was on my way to the kitchen to grab a soda. Do you want one?"

"Yeah, that would be great. So, what do want to do today?" Jeff asked her.

"I was thinking that since you will be leaving this weekend that we could just hang out here without any friends around. Maybe listen to some music up in my room," Felicia suggested. She really didn't want to share her time with Jeff with anyone else. Felicia hoped he wouldn't think of her idea as boring and decide to leave.

"That sounds great," he reassured her.

"Cool. Follow me," Felicia told him as she handed him a Pepsi from the fridge. Felicia led the way upstairs to her bedroom. As they entered, she turned on her stereo and noticed that Jeff had closed the door. She briefly thought about the rule of the house, of how she wasn't allowed to have guys in the house when parents weren't home, let alone have them in her room with the door closed even when they *were* there. She quickly dismissed the thought. Her parents wouldn't be home for a while and since her room overlooked the driveway, she could see when they drove up. It would give her plenty of time to get Jeff out of her room, which would be the bigger problem than just having him over. Felicia had already had a plan in her mind on how to explain why he was there without parents in the house.

Felicia kicked off her canary yellow sandals and sat Indian style on her bed. Jeff grabbed the stack of CDs next to her stereo and sat in the mushroom chair next to the bed. For the next thirty minutes, they sat and chatted about the upcoming school year. While Felicia was looking forward to being a senior in high school, she wasn't looking forward to Jeff going back to St. Peters, and said as much to him.

"I'm really going to miss you after you leave," Felicia sighed with a little sadness in her voice.

"We will stay in touch. I have your number, and I can come up to visit on the weekends," Jeff reassured her.

"I know, but it just won't be the same," she continued. "I just wish you lived here. I've really enjoyed my summer with you. You are a really great guy."

"Well, I think you are pretty special, too," Jeff said as he stood up and moved over to sit next to her on the bed. He leaned over and gave her a kiss. Felicia kissed him back wholeheartedly. His kisses always made her mind fuzzy, and she liked how he made her feel beautiful.

Suddenly, the tone of Jeff's kisses changed. Felicia realized that they were no longer sitting on the bed. Instead, she was lying down with Jeff above her. *When did that happen?* Felicia thought to herself. Jeff was kissing her harder, mashing her mouth against her teeth. *This isn't right.* She started to get nervous. The nervousness turned to fear as Jeff started touching her in places she had never dreamed she would be touched, places she didn't want to be touched. As he started kissing her neck, Felicia whispered, "No, Jeff. I don't want this." She tried to swallow down the fear that was rising in her throat. She didn't want him to know how scared she was.

"Shhh," Jeff whispered in her ear, "trust me, Felicia. You'll like this." Jeff continued with kissing her neck and touching her all over. The kisses were no longer the soft kisses that she enjoyed so much, the ones that made her knees weak. And the touches were not a caress, the kind she always read about in her romance books.

Felicia was more scared than she had ever been. She started shaking her head. "No, I don't want to do this." Tears started streaming down her cheeks. "Please, stop. Please."

"Come on, Felicia. You know you want to do this. Trust me, it will be fine." Jeff continued on, ignoring her quiet pleas and the tears.

Felicia had stiffened her whole body, terrified of what was about to happen. In her mind she was screaming *No!* over and over, but she couldn't seem to get the word out. So, she continued to shake her head and mutter "no." Just as Jeff started to unbutton his pants there was a knock on Felicia's bedroom door. Felicia took the opportunity to sit up as she looked at the door. She glanced from the door to Jeff's face and saw irritation in his eyes as he grimaced at the intrusion. He started to button his pants back up as Felicia got up to answer the door. It was then when she realized her skirt had been pushed up and her underwear was down to her ankles. Caught up in the fear of what was about to happen, it never registered in Felicia's mind what all Jeff had been doing. She quickly made herself presentable and walked to the door. Never before was she so thankful for an intrusion on her privacy.

She opened the door to find Allison on the other side. It took all of her control not to throw her arms around her sister. She could have kissed her for knocking when she did. Felicia must have looked pale because the first thing out of Allison's mouth was, "Are you all right?" Felicia could see the concern in her face.

Felicia put on the brightest smile she could muster and said, "Sure, everything is fine. We are just listening to some music."

"Well, you are lucky Mom and Dad aren't here. And just so you know, they are on their way home," Allison informed her younger sister.

Felicia turned to Jeff, "I guess you had better go." Inside she was relieved she had an excuse for him to leave.

"Yeah, I guess I better go," Jeff said as he walked toward her. Felicia tried not to stiffen her body as he gave her a hug.

"I'll call you later," Felicia told him as he walked downstairs.

"Yeah, whatever," he tossed over his shoulder as he let himself out the front door.

Felicia turned back to Allison to find her looking at her strangely. "What?" she asked.

"Nothing. Did I interrupt something?" Allison asked her.

There was no way Felicia was going to tell her what happened. She planned to keep the day's events to herself for as long as she lived. "No, why do you ask?" Felicia responded, trying to look as casual as she could.

"Because you still look pale and the look on your face when you opened the door."

"Oh, that. It was nothing. Jeff and I were having a small argument when you knocked, and I was glad to have an excuse to stop arguing." Felicia felt the lie tripping out of her mouth with ease. She knew that she would just die if her sister, or anyone else, found out the truth.

"OK, if you say so." Allison didn't look too convinced. "Well, the reason I knocked was to see if I could borrow the pink diamond necklace for this weekend. I have a date and that necklace would go perfectly with my outfit."

"Yeah, no problem. Let me get it for you." Felicia quickly found the necklace and practically shoved her sister out of her room. She wanted nothing more than to be alone for a while. And the last thing she needed was for Allison to stand there and scrutinize her every move and emotion that crossed her face. As she shut her door, Felicia finally collapsed to the floor, quiet sobs wracking her body.

Chapter 9

It was some time later before Felicia got up off the floor and went to her desk. She looked at herself in the mirror and saw puffy, red eyes staring back at her. She didn't recognize the girl she saw. The girl in the mirror was someone who still had fear and uncertainty running across her face. *What am I going do now? I've probably lost a wonderful boyfriend.* Felicia thought to herself. *Wonderful?* Her mind argued with her heart. *What was wonderful about what he did? He didn't listen to you when you said 'no'.* But Felicia's heart thought otherwise.

She felt the war in her, felt it tearing her apart. She knew her heart was right. She knew that if she hadn't brought him up to the room he wouldn't have thought it was OK to try anything. If she hadn't worn the outfit she was wearing, he wouldn't have been provoked. All of the "ifs" kept running through her mind until she thought her head would explode. *I gotta get out of here.* Felicia quickly changed clothes, tossing on her jogging shorts and shirt. As soon as she had her shoes on she was running down the steps hollering, "I'm going for a run!" to anyone who was listening. If no one heard, she didn't care. All she cared about was getting out of the house.

When she returned home, it was getting close to dinnertime. She had come to the decision that no one was to ever know about what happened. She would add that to her little pile of secrets, which were quickly becoming a big pile. She just hoped that one day that pile of secrets wouldn't overtake her. Felicia knew that if her friends, or anyone in school for that matter, found out about today they would call her a prude and a tease, and she would never have another boyfriend. She just hoped she hadn't lost this boyfriend.

She passed the kitchen as she started up the stairs. Felicia hoped to get past it before her mom saw her. She still wasn't in the mood to be around anyone. No such luck.

"Felicia, after you change, please come down here and help me get dinner on the table," her mom hollered at her.

Felicia quietly sighed. At least her mom would think the red, blotchy face was from running and not crying, sparing her from a round of questions she didn't feel like answering. "OK, Mom. I'll be down in a minute," Felicia answered as she jogged up the steps.

Felicia quickly splashed her face with cold water to help the puffiness around her eyes. She climbed into her comfortable St. Louis Blues sweats and sweatshirt, her favorite gift from Cy, and headed downstairs to help her mom. She prayed the whole way there that her mom wouldn't question her about the day. She never planned to talk about the actual events, and her heart wasn't into making up stories right at the moment.

"So what are we having for dinner tonight?" Felicia asked as she walked into the kitchen. She always loved the kitchen, hated the chores that went with it, but loved the smells. It always reminded her of family and being loved. She took a deep breath, letting her nose fill with the smells of spices of coriander, all spice, dill, and cloves, which always brought the memories of shrimp. Since shrimp was one of her favorite meals, she was hoping for that was being fixed. She could use a night of her favorite comfort food.

"Well, your father and I decided it has been a long time since we had a seafood-night, so I've put on a big pot of shrimp and crab legs," her mother said as she tossed a few more spices in with the shrimp. "Why don't you start on the corn?"

"Cool, I am ready for a good seafood-night!" Felicia told her mom as she started shucking the corn. One thing about her family that she liked was that they believed in eating fresh foods. It always tasted better than the frozen, so she never truly minded the extra preparation.

Once Felicia had the corn cooking she went to set the table. The activity helped her shove what happened earlier that day into the back of her mind. *This is what I need to do. I need to stay busy and just shove that whole incident behind me. I made a mistake and hopefully Jeff will understand.*

Dinner was uneventful. Thankfully, her parents didn't ask any questions about her day, and Allison kept all of her opinions to herself. She did catch her sister staring at her a couple of times. Felicia made a point to ignore her.

Felicia was exhausted by the time she climbed the steps to her bedroom. She heard the wind pick up and shuddered. *Great, just great,* she thought to herself. *This is just what I need after the day I've had, another freaking storm.* She hoped it wouldn't be a bad one, she needed sleep tonight. She started to enter her dark room but paused in the doorway. She reached her arm around the wall and felt for the light switch and then flicked on the light, glancing around the room, before she entered. She shook her head at herself. What was she thinking? Did she think there would be somebody hiding in her room? Felicia snorted in disgust with herself. Once again, she felt as if she was being a big baby about the incoming storm.

She quickly changed into her fuzzy pink pajamas, the one that made her feel safe and were very comfortable. Grabbing her favorite stuffed white bear, she crawled in bed and pulled the covers up to her ears. She always felt safest with her back and neck covered. Strange, yes, but it was the only way she could go to sleep, especially with a storm brewing.

Felicia lay in bed waiting for sleep to overtake her. However, each time she closed her eyes she relived the events of that afternoon. *This is ridiculous!* Felicia chided herself. *Grow up, Felicia! Put this behind you and all will be OK.* With those thoughts she closed her eyes and tried to think of her favorite place. She pictured herself on a beach with white sand stretching for miles, glistening in the afternoon sunlight. She could hear the waves crashing softly on the shore, just touching her toes as she stretched out basking in the warmth of the sand beneath her and the sun above. Felicia let the thoughts of warmth surround her and lull her to sleep. Snuggling up to the bear, she finally relaxed enough to let the fear drain from her body and drift off to sleep, hoping that tomorrow would be a better day.

Chapter 10

As each day came and went, Felicia didn't hear from Jeff. She knew he was leaving that weekend and hoped to see him one more time, if only just to tell him how much she adored him and hoped they could continue their relationship. She just knew that the distance between the towns wouldn't get in the way of true love.

She woke up late Thursday morning to the sound of her cell phone ringing. She jumped out of bed and ran to grab it, hoping it was Jeff. It was Celia. She tried not to let the disappointment sound in her voice as she answered. "Hey, Celia! Long time no hear. What have you been up to this past week?"

"Oh, not much. Cole has been a total jerk all week. We've done nothing but fight, and I'm tired of it. I was thinking, how about going to *The Vortex* with me tonight?"

Celia sounded so hopeful that Felicia couldn't bear to tell her no. Plus, maybe Jeff would be there. She knew he liked to dance, and that was the only teen dance club in town. "Sure, sounds like a great idea. Maybe Jeff will be there. I haven't heard from him all week. I'm sure he has been busy with getting ready to go back home this weekend," Felicia said, continuing to make excuses in her mind for Jeff's failures. "What time will you be by?"

"Awesome!" shrieked Celia. "I totally need this girl's night out. And if you haven't heard from Jeff, then you need a girl's night out as well."

Felicia couldn't argue with that observation. She knew she could use some girlfriend time. Grinning into the phone, Felicia asked again, "So, what time are ya picking me up?"

"Oh, yeah! Um, how about around 8:00? You know that the dance club doesn't really get going until 8:30 or 9. We could always pick up something to drink before we go," Celia suggested.

"Sounds like a plan," Felicia said knowing that the drink that Celia talked about wasn't Mountain Dew. While *The Vortex* didn't allow alcohol, most teens knew who would buy for them and how to sneak it inside. Water bottles and cups from a fast-food joint were rarely questioned. "I'll see ya around 8:00!" Felicia realized as she closed her cell phone that she was actually excited about going. *Maybe Celia is right, and this is exactly what I need—a girl's night out. And if Jeff happens to be there, it will be an added bonus.* Smiling a true smile the first time in a few days, Felicia began to pick out her outfit for the night.

Around 8:00, Felicia went downstairs to find her mom and dad. She felt the best that she had since the whole incident with Jeff had happened. She was wearing her favorite pair of Levi Capris, the kind that made her feel skinner than she truly was. She decided to wear a pink V-front T-shirt that showed off her curves. Silver earrings, necklace, and dolphin bracelet finished off her outfit. She felt absolutely beautiful. She slipped into her sandals and placed a toe ring on her third toe and considered herself completely dressed for the night.

Felicia found her parents playing Hand and Foot, their favorite card game, in the kitchen. "I'm going to *The Vortex* with Celia tonight. I should be home around 11:00, or 12:00, if that is OK with you." Her parents had relaxed some on the curfew this summer, and for that, Felicia was eternally grateful.

"Sure, Sweetie, that sounds fine," her mom told her. "Have a great time," she encouraged her as she lay down her last card in her "Hand" and picked up her "Foot."

"I'm sure you will have more fun than I am," grumbled her dad. "Your mom is killing me in this game."

Felicia laughed at her parents. "Dad, I don't know why you continue to play this game with Mom. You know she will beat you every time."

Her dad looked up at her with a twinkle in his gray eyes, "Ah, but you see, I let her win most of the games. It keeps the peace in the house."

Felicia's mom rolled her eyes, "Oh, Carl, you are so full of it!" As she laid a queen down and created yet another book, her mom giggled like a teenager.

The doorbell rang, signaling that Celia was there to get Felicia. Laughing at her parents, she gave them each a hug and headed toward the front door.

"Wow, you look awesome!" Felicia exclaimed as she opened the door and saw Celia. She was wearing her blue jean mini-skirt, an aqua tank layered with a yellow tank, and gold hoop earrings, necklace, and ankle bracelet. Gold always looked good on Celia. It complimented her sun-kissed skin.

"Thanks, so do you," grinned Celia. "Are ya ready to go?"

"You bet! I am ready to have a little bit of fun." With that, the girls headed out to Celia's car. As Felicia slid into the passenger seat, she once again envied Celia for having a car to use on a regular basis.

Celia drove by John's house, a sure bet of getting alcohol. Felicia and Celia ran up the front steps and knocked on the door. John's older brother answered the door and told them they could find him upstairs in the game room.

"Hey, John," Celia hollered as they entered the room. They saw him playing pool with a couple of his friends. Felicia recognized them as students from the local college.

"Hey! What are you girls up to tonight?" John shot the seven ball into the side pocket.

"We are on our way to *The Vortex* and decided we were in need of more than just a virgin daiquiri," Celia explained. "Have anything you can spare?"

Felicia held her tongue as the two continued to talk. She really had no desire to drink, but she wasn't going to keep Celia from getting the alcohol.

They continued to chat with John and his friends for a while longer before heading off to the club. When they arrived, the place was beginning to get crowded. Felicia scanned the cars in the parking lot looking for Jeff's truck. She felt her heart sink a little when she realized it wasn't there. Determined to make the most of the evening, though, she put a smile on her face and entered the dance club with Celia.

The noise of the music and talking assaulted Felicia's senses. She loved the feel of the beat of the music; it always gave her the energy to dance. They instantly headed to the dance floor and joined a group of friends that were dancing in the middle. The latest Linkin Park song was blaring through the many speakers that surrounded the dance floor. The beat of the song helped Felicia forget her troubles. *This is the best part of dancing; I can always just lose myself in the music.* As the song ended, another one began—a classic from AC/DC. Felicia stayed out on the dance floor until the first slow song came on. She caught Celia's eye and motioned with her head that she was going to sit out for a few minutes. Celia, dancing with someone Felicia didn't recognize, nodded her head in acknowledgment and continued the slow dance.

Felicia found a table close to the dance floor. She caught herself looking through the crowd and realized that she was keeping an eye out for Jeff. The slower music didn't help her mood. No Jeff meant that there would be no slow dancing, no last good-byes, and no boyfriend.

After about another hour, Felicia decided she had had enough. Celia was acting stupid due to the alcohol she had hidden in her purse. Jeff was nowhere to be found, and she really wasn't having that great of a time. She caught up with Celia on the dance floor. "Hey, I need to get out of here," she shouted over the music.

"Um, OK, you can take my car. Rob can give me a lift home," Celia pointed in the general direction of the guy she was dancing with at the moment, a sure sign Celia had way too much to drink.

"Are you sure about that?" Felicia was concerned since she had never seen this guy before.

"Yeah, no problem. I can take Celia anywhere she wants to go," responded the guy, who Celia called Rob.

"OK, call me if you need me to come get you," Felicia said as she gave Celia a quick hug. Even though she was slightly concerned for Celia, she felt the need to get out of there plus Celia was old enough to take care of herself.

Felicia slowly walked toward Celia's car, wondering if she would ever see Jeff. *All of this mess is my fault,* she kept saying over and over in her head. By the time she reached the car, tears were flowing freely down her face. *I can't even keep a decent boyfriend.* Felicia knew that these thoughts were probably ridiculous, but she couldn't keep them from coming.

She reached the car and glanced up at the windshield before she walked around to the side. Stuck in between the wiper and the glass was a piece of paper with her name scrawled across the front. She recognized the handwriting as Jeff's. Quickly snatching the note off the windshield, Felicia felt her hopes rise. *Maybe he wants to meet me somewhere. I'm sure that is why he isn't here; he wanted to meet me in private so we can say our good-byes without an audience.* Feeling more lighthearted, Felicia eagerly opened the note. It wasn't very long, actually contained only one sentence. But, that one sentence resounded loudly in her mind. She couldn't believe what she was reading and read it over and over just to be sure she read it correctly.

It definitely was from Jeff, but it didn't say what she hoped it did. In his bold, messy scrawl, he had written

Felicia You're not
Worth it!

Jeff

Chapter 11

Felicia felt as though she was punched in the stomach, and time began to stand still. Jeff's words resounded loud and clear in her head over and over, "Felicia, you're not worth it." She knew exactly what he meant. He meant that she wasn't worth having as a girlfriend, as a friend, or as anything. He verified everything she had ever felt in her life, she was worthless.

Walking as if in a dream, she climbed into Celia's car. She sat there for a few moments not knowing where to go or what to do. Starting the car, she decided to just drive around and see if she could clear the whirling thoughts out of her mind. Thirty minutes later, she found herself at a lookout that many teens went to on the weekends. Thankfully, it was early enough and no one was there. Unsure of how she got there, but grateful that she found a peaceful place, she slowly got out of the car to go sit on an outcropping that looked over a river.

Felicia sat there staring out into space trying to figure out what to do next. She was positive that Jeff dumped her because of the incident in her bedroom. *This is all my fault.* Felicia's mind kept going around and around that phrase, remembering how Jeff had said she wasn't worth it. She was worthless, and this just solidified what she had always thought. She was afraid of storms, afraid of being a failure, and kept so many secrets locked in her that she knew that Jeff was right. But, why if he was so right did she still get nervous when she walked in her room at night? *I guess that is just more of how I am worthless.*

With that last thought, Felicia's tears came, freely flowing down her face. She sat on the rock with her knees up to her chin. Burying her face into her knees, she began to sob, the kind of sobs that shook her body.

Felicia didn't know how long she sat there crying, but eventually she began to notice the hard, mossy rock she was sitting on as well as the chill in the air. Shivering, she straightened up and glanced out across the river. The full moon lent enough light for her to see the water flowing over the rocks. At that moment, she heard a twig snap in the woods next to her. She suddenly realized just how alone she was at the lookout. Her heart felt as if it was in her throat as she looked around to see if it was an animal that made the noise. She couldn't make anything out other than shadows. Trying to convince herself that it was nothing more than a squirrel, she tried to relax again.

Another twig snapped, and Felicia jumped up looking around. Her fear had finally taken control of her whole body. She forgot about being chilled and decided that it was time for her to get out of there. Running back to the car, she opened the front door and checked the back seats before sliding into the driver's seat. She quickly locked all of the doors, turned the key in the ignition praying that it would start. As the car roared to life, Felicia slammed it into reverse and left the lookout as if the devil were at her heels.

Deciding to just drive on home, reasoning with herself that she can just take Celia's car back to her tomorrow, Felicia turned the car in that direction. As she pulled up to her house, she noticed that all of the lights were on in the living room. "Great, just great," muttered Felicia. Checking her face in the mirror, coming to the conclusion there was nothing she could do about the puffy eyes and blotchy face, she decided that she would go straight to her room hoping that no one stepped into her path. She really wasn't up for questions.

Felicia let herself in the front door, locking it behind her. Noticing her parents in the living room, Felicia hollered, "I'm home and going to bed," as she headed for the stairs.

"Felicia!" The sound of her mother's voice stopped her in her tracks.

She had almost made it to the steps and was going to be home free. She turned and walked back to the living room entrance. "Yes, Mom?" Felicia was quite proud of herself; her voice was even, and no one would be able to tell she had been crying.

"Your father and I just wanted to know if you had a good time," her mom explained.

"Oh, yeah, had a great time. Thanks for asking." Felicia started back toward the steps when her dad's voice stopped her.

"We noticed that you drove Celia's car, but Celia is not with you. What is up with that?" He didn't sound angry, but he did sound as if he wanted a truthful answer.

Felicia briefly thought about telling them the truth about Celia's drinking, Jeff's note, and how horrible she felt. But, she was too afraid her parents would be disappointed in her—assume she drank the alcohol, and wonder why Jeff wrote such a note to break it off. And *that* was not an issue she wanted to discuss. So, she quickly came up with a story she knew her parents would believe. "Well, Celia got sick while we were at *The Vortex*. Since she couldn't drive because of the stomach cramps, I drove her home. She told me to just take her car on to my house and bring it back tomorrow, when hopefully she is feeling better. Since it was fairly late for her parents, they agreed with her."

Felicia held her breath as her father stared at her. She was positive he could read right through her lies. Finally, he nodded his head, "OK. Well, I'm glad you were there to help her out. We'll make sure her car gets back to her tomorrow."

Silently letting out her breath, she said her good nights and headed upstairs. As she opened her bedroom door, she discovered that once again, she couldn't walk in without turning on the light. *This is absolutely stupid*, Felicia chided herself. But, she couldn't seem to bring herself to walk into a dark room anymore. Once again, reaching around the wall she flipped on the light and turned on her stereo to her favorite classical music station, then began to change into her pajamas. After slipping into her fuzzy, pink pajama bottoms and top, she grabbed her brush and brushed her hair until it was as smooth as silk. She brushed her teeth, turned on the lamp beside her bed, and only then turned off the light to her room.

Lately, she discovered that she couldn't get to sleep in a dark room. The pure darkness, the kind where you can't see your hand in front of your face, brought fear to Felicia. The fear would build until it was in her throat and she felt like she could just scream. So, she would turn on the lamp by her bed and listen to classical music to help her fall asleep. Usually, this would help ward off the nightmares she had in the past month. But tonight, nothing seemed to help. As she closed her eyes, the note Jeff wrote seemed to become life-size in her mind and the words she detested the most resounded in her mind over and over, *you're not worth it, not worth it, not worth it, not worth it.* She finally fell asleep with those words running through her mind.

Chapter 12

Summer was quickly winding down; school started in just a week. Felicia was out shopping with her mom for school clothes, not one of Felicia's favorite things to do. She loved shopping, just not with her mom. Everything she picked out her mom would wrinkle her nose and tell her that "no proper young lady would wear something like *that*." Usually, these shopping trips turned into one long day of fight after fight. And today was no different.

"How about this one," her mom held up a very elementary-girlish top—pink with the latest Disney girl idol on it.

Rolling her eyes Felicia responded with, "Only when hell freezes over." Lately, she found herself caring less and less what her parents thought of her language.

Her mother gave her a stony look, piercing Felicia with her golden brown tiger-eyes. "I do not appreciate that kind of language, young lady, and you well know it."

Felicia just shrugged and walked toward the juniors section of the store. She knew her mother would follow her, so she didn't even glance back. While sifting through a sale rack, the hairs on the back of her neck prickled as if someone was watching her. Felicia glanced around quickly, but only saw her mom close by. She shook her head and chided herself. She was starting to imagine things, now. However, all day she couldn't shake that feeling that someone was watching, following her.

By the time Felicia and her mom got home, Felicia was worn out. Not only was she worn out from all of the fights, but she was also tired of looking over her shoulder. She caught herself doing that several times in the different stores they went to in the mall.

As they walked through the door, Felicia heard her father holler from the living room, "So, how did the infamous shopping trip go."

"Fine," Felicia hollered back and quickly retreated to her room where she slammed the door and turned on some music. She turned it up loud enough so that if a freight train went by, she couldn't hear it. She hoped that the loud noise would drown out the fears she had that was coursing through her body.

Her mom walked into the living room, sighed and sat down in her favorite overstuffed leather armchair. "I don't know what has gotten into Felicia, Carl. She was outright disrespectful toward me." She then explained in great detail all of the fights that occurred throughout the day.

"It's as if she isn't herself anymore. I just don't know what to do," Mary commented.

"Well, she is a senior this coming year, and teens do change each year. I agree that it is unusual for her to be so blatantly disrespectful toward you. However, let's give it some time before we do anything. Maybe it is just a phase."

His reply to the concerns would have been shocking to Felicia if she had heard them. He usually took the hard line with her, and even Felicia's mom seemed shocked by his response. But she agreed to just give it some time to see if Felicia would become "herself" again.

Upstairs, blasting music from her favorite rock band, Felicia put away her new clothes and gathered her school supplies. Finally she was facing her senior year. *I can't wait to get out of this house!* Felicia was more than ready to move away to go to college. She was already accepted to Alabama State University. She still wasn't sure what she wanted to major in, but at this point she didn't care. She just wanted to move away, as far away as possible. Luckily, the university was several hours away so once she moved Felicia wouldn't have to worry about her parents just "dropping in" on her, which she knew they would definitely do. Oh, they promised her that they would never do that, but she wouldn't put anything past those prison wardens.

As she was hanging up her tops, she felt the buzz of her cell phone in her pocket. Looking at the screen she saw that Celia had sent her a text. She hadn't talked to Celia in a couple of weeks. It seemed that ever since the incident with Jeff happened she didn't talk to Celia or any of her friends anymore. She blamed the lack of communication on her friends, telling herself that they just didn't bother to text or call her anymore. Obviously, she wasn't worth talking to.

She slid open her phone and read the text, "Hey girl! Call me! Haven't talked for a long time. Got some things to tell ya!"

Felicia thought about calling Celia right then, but decided she wasn't in the mood to talk to her right now; so, she texted back, "OK. Busy right now . . . will call later." When she felt the buzz of her phone again, she didn't bother looking at it.

Just then she heard pounding on the door. Felicia yanked it open to find Josh on the other side, looking disgusted. "Mom and dad said to turn that stereo down, the neighbors are complaining about the noise."

"Ha, ha, ha," she responded as she turned the volume down.

"Oh, and dinner is ready."

"Tell them I'm not hungry," Felicia said honestly. She wasn't that hungry and really didn't feel like dealing with her family. She knew Allison would be over for dinner, and she *really* didn't want to hear how great "rush week" went at her sorority.

Josh shrugged and said, "OK, but they won't like it."

Felicia knew they wouldn't like it. Her dad was always telling them, "A family eats together at the table, and the whole family should be there unless you are on your deathbed." Of course, once you moved away to college you were exempt from that rule. Allison always came over because she was close and she liked to suck up to their parents. Felicia really didn't care if they liked it or not. She found she didn't care about much, anymore.

Just as she suspected, her mom was at her door in less than two minutes after Josh left. Opening the door to her soft knock, Felicia told her, "I know the rules, Mom, but I really am not hungry. I don't feel too good. I think I'm coming down with something." Felicia knew that pulling the "sick card" usually works, and her mom didn't disappoint her.

Mary gave her a concerned look, touched her forehead with the back of her hand, and said, "Well, you do look a little pale. OK, lie down, and I'll bring some soup up in a little bit, if you feel up to eating it."

"Thanks," Felicia said. Really, her mom wasn't all that bad. She just had some quirky ideas about clothing.

For the first time in a week, Felicia did what she was told. As she laid on her bed she discovered that she was really more tired than she thought. She pulled her St. Louis Blues fleece throw, that Cy had given her last Christmas, over her and closed her eyes. Her mind went back over the day's events; the fights with her mom and the uneasiness she felt all day while shopping. *Maybe I ought to tell Cy about the feeling that I'm being followed and watched.* Felicia thought through the idea. In some ways it sounded like a good idea, but in many ways it was a very bad idea.

If she told Cy what she was feeling then he might think she was crazy or worse yet ask her if something had happened to create this uneasiness. She was positive that nothing had happened that would make her feel as if someone was following her, but he was good at questioning people, and he might eventually figure out her secret about Jeff. And *that* was something that he could never find out.

Chapter 13

The first day of school came with an unusual heat wave. Thankfully, their building was one of the newer ones in the county and they had air-conditioning. As Felicia walked to her locker, she saw Celia. Quickly, she glanced away. She wasn't up to Celia's questions or dramatics. Celia saw her, though, and dodging through the students in the crowded senior hallway, she made her way to Felicia.

"Hey, I've texted you a thousand times and left several voice mails lately, and you haven't called me back. What's the deal?" Celia looked more concerned than mad.

For some reason, the look in Celia's eyes put Felicia on the defensive. "I've been busy, Celia. I can't drop what I'm doing to call or text you every time you call." Felicia caught the hurt that crossed Celia's eyes. If she hadn't been looking at her in the face, she would have missed it. She wished she hadn't been looking. Seeing the hurt just made her feel all that more bad about how she was acting.

She started to apologize but Celia stopped her. "OK, fine. I can tell when you need your space. Obviously, you need it now. I'll try not to bug you." And with that last comment, Celia left.

Felicia watched her as she blended into the crowd. *Great,* Felicia thought, *I've just lost my best friend. God, Felicia, you are so stupid. You can't even keep a good friend.* Felicia slammed her locker door shut and went to her first hour class. *What a way to start my senior year.*

She walked into her math class, headed for the last row, and slid into a seat next to someone she didn't know. She wasn't up to sitting next to those that she used to sit next to—the gossip and talk of the summer would be too much for her. As the hour droned on, Felicia felt the hairs on her neck go on end. The fear in her started to rise, and she felt the uncontrollable need to leave the room. By the time the bell rang, she was short of breath. All she could think about was getting out of there and away from the crowded classrooms and hallway.

She moved through the hallway to her next class as if she was in a dream. Continuously looking around, for what she didn't know, she reached her next class and chose a desk in the back of the room with her back facing the wall. Felicia was ready to get this day over. The start of her senior year was nothing like she thought it would be.

By the time the three o'clock bell rang, Felicia's nerves were shot. She walked out to the parking lot and headed toward her car. She started to climb into the driver's seat when she heard someone call her name. She turned to see the girl she sat next to in her math class jogging over to her car.

"Hey, Felicia, I'm Calli. I sit next to you in math class," Calli said brushing her dark hair out of her eyes.

"Yeah, I remember seeing you," Felicia said looking at her curiously.

"Well, I was wondering if you could give me a ride home. I missed my bus," Calli explained.

Felicia opened her mouth to tell her that she couldn't give her a ride since her car was a "to and from school use only" car. She shut her mouth and thought for a minute. *What will it hurt if I give her a ride home? I'm a senior this year, and I should have more privileges.* Felicia looked at Calli and said, "Sure, not a problem. Hop on in."

"Thanks," Calli said with a grin.

Felicia and Calli chatted about who they each had for their classes that year. Felicia decided that she liked Calli, even if she did dress differently than others. She knew that her parents wouldn't approve just because of the way Calli was dressed. They had something against people who wore heavy makeup and dark clothing. In school they were called "Goths" but Felicia realized that Calli was just like her.

Felicia pulled up to Calli's house and as Calli opened the door Felicia told her to call her anytime she needed a ride. They really didn't live that far from each other. After saying good-bye, Felicia headed for home.

As she pulled up in the driveway, she saw her mom's car. *Wonderful* Felicia thought to herself *just what I need, an inquisition about my day.* Slowly getting out of the car, Felicia looked toward the house contemplating on whether or not to go inside. Suddenly, she felt as if someone was watching her again. Feeling the goose bumps crawl up her arms, she chose to go inside, inquisition or not. Slamming the car door behind her, she ran up to the house and hurried inside.

Glancing into the living room she saw her little brother playing on the X-Box. She assumed her mom must be in the kitchen getting dinner ready. Walking as quietly as she could, Felicia headed upstairs to her bedroom. She opened her door and let out the breath she had been holding.

Her luck held out until dinnertime. Josh pounded on her door to let her know, dinner was ready. Taking a deep breath she headed downstairs.

Dinner wasn't as bad as she thought it would be. She was able to answer her parents' questions with the minimal "not much" and "yeah, I guess so." As soon as she could she went back to her room to listen to more music. She fell asleep listening to some classic AC/DC music.

She awoke the next day to the buzzing of her phone. Assuming it was Celia, she hit the ignore button. A minute later her phone buzzed again. Glancing at the caller *ID* she realized that it was a number she didn't know.

"Hello?" Felicia answered, still not fully awake.

"Hey, Felicia, it's Calli. I was wondering if you could give me a ride to school today."

Waking up fully, Felicia sat up in her bed. "Hey, Calli. Sure that won't be a problem." She glanced at the clock and realized it was later than she thought. She would have to hustle if she was going to pick Calli up. "Um, I can be there in about thirty minutes if that is OK."

"Yeah, sure. Thanks, Felicia!" Calli said.

As soon as Felicia hung up the phone, she darted off her bed and toward her closet. Tossing her hair up in a pony tail, she grabbed a pair of jeans and T-shirt. She was on her way out the door when her mom stopped her in the entry way.

"Felicia, you are in a hurry this morning. Have you had your breakfast yet?" her mom asked.

"No, I haven't had breakfast, but I'm not that hungry. I'll grab something at school. I'm supposed to meet someone at school this morning before classes start," Felicia told her mom.

"Oh, OK. Well then, have a good day, Sweetheart." Her mom reached out to give her a hug, but Felicia slid by her before she had a chance.

Once at school, Felicia and Calli met up again in the first hour. Calli was telling her of an upcoming party that weekend when the teacher asked for the homework assigned the night before. Felicia realized that she didn't touch any of her homework the night before. Shrugging off any guilty thoughts, Felicia continued talking to Calli.

"So, the group I hang with is having a 'back-to-school bash' Friday night. The whole back-to-school thing is a big joke, though. Half of the guys have already graduated. They just find any excuse to have a party." Calli explained. "Do you want to come along?"

"Yeah, that sounds like fun. I'll see if I can get the car this weekend. My parents have been a big pain about letting me drive besides going to and from school. But, I'm a senior this year, and my older sister was allowed to drive on the weekends her senior year. So, I should have a good argument." Felicia was already formulating the argument in her head.

"Cool," Calli said. At that point, the teacher gave both girls "the look." Calli and Felicia both rolled their eyes, but then quieted down.

That night, Felicia brought up the weekend driving to her parents. Gearing up for a battle, Felicia told them, "Since

I'm a senior this year I should be allowed to drive on the weekends."

It was much to Felicia's surprise when her dad answered with, "You are right, Felicia. You have proven that you can be responsible so you will be allowed to have the car."

Felicia couldn't believe her ears. *Well, that was easy,* she thought to herself. As she started to turn away, silently celebrating, she heard her dad say, "But, one sign of irresponsibility and the car is ours." Felicia sighed. She knew it would have been too good to be true if they just gave her the car keys and said, "Go, be free, and have fun."

That Friday night she picked Calli up and they headed toward the apartments where "the gang" hung out. Felicia walked into the apartment to find a mixture of age groups, as well as a mixture of activities going on. Some were sitting around having a mini-jam session with their acoustic guitars while others were playing games on the X-Box. Everyone had a drink in their hands. To Felicia's pleasant surprise, they had more than just beer to drink. Felicia had one of the guys, Joe she thought his name was, pour her a glass of Absolute Vodka and set to visit with Calli and her friends.

Before she knew it, her curfew had come and gone. *Oh well,* Felicia thought, *like I care about curfews anymore.* She finally decided to head home around 2 a.m. She found Calli, made sure she had a ride home, and said her good-byes to her newfound friends.

Felicia drove home a little slower than she normally would have, knowing the cops would be out, and she had had several glasses of vodka. When she pulled up in the darkened driveway, she let out a breath of relief. Quietly, she went into the house and snuck up to her room. Felicia crashed on her bed and felt the world tilt a bit. She closed her eyes and finally the world stopped tilting and whirling, and she was able to fall asleep.

~*~*~*~*~*~*~*~*~*~*~

Felicia was in her first hour when the announcements came on in school.

"Good morning! We have come to the three-week mark in our first semester. You know what this means, everyone will be receiving progress reports from their teachers. Be sure to take them home to your parents."

Yeah, right, thought Felicia, *as if I am going to show them my grades.* Without even looking at her progress reports, Felicia knew they weren't going to be the best. She spent most of her day writing notes to Calli about the party they went to or the party coming up. She had no desire to do any school work, and she wasn't about to change that for a few measly good grades to make her parents happy. As she received her progress reports in each class, she promptly shoved them into the deep dark recesses of her backpack.

After school, while walking with Calli to her car, Felicia ran into Celia. She hadn't talked to Celia since the first day of school.

"Hey Felicia," Celia greeted her with a warm smile. "I've been wondering about you. How are you doing? I haven't talked to you in forever!"

"Oh, hi, Celia," Felicia briefly paused to greet her old friend but tried to give her the impression that she wasn't in the mood to stand around and chat. Obviously, Celia either didn't catch on or was ignoring that fact for she continued to talk.

"So, how is school going this year? I just got my grades and my parents are going to kill me. I made a C in math, again. You would think they would be used to this by now." Celia grinned at Felicia, hoping to get some kind of friendly response.

"Um, yeah. School is fine and I guess my grades are OK. I really didn't look at them. I'm pretty sure I'm failing math. It's boring and I figure I won't use most of what they are teaching me anyway. Look, we have to split. We are supposed to be meeting some friends down at *The Cave*." And with that, Felicia and Calli headed off toward the car.

Celia stared after Felicia with concern in her eyes. "What has happened to her," Celia wondered out loud. "She is definitely not acting like herself and hasn't for a while." And with thoughts of Felicia on her mind, Celia headed for home.

Chapter 14

Celia pulled into the grocery store parking lot; she had promised her mom that she would pick up some items for dinner that night. As she pulled into a parking spot, she noticed the car next to her looked familiar. It was an unmarked police car. Secretly hoping it belonged to Captain Leathers, she hurried into the store.

As she walked toward the bakery section of the grocery store, Celia kept her eye out for Captain Leathers. If anyone could help her figure out this problem, Leathers would be the one. Luck was with her, she spotted him in the chip aisle. Walking toward him, Celia causally called out, "Hey, Captain Leathers!"

Leathers turned to see who was calling him and grinned when he saw Celia. He was familiar with Felicia's best friend, having spent many Monday nights watching football over at the Morgan household. And generally, Celia would be hanging out with Felicia at the Morgan's house. "Hey, Kiddo. Haven't seen you in a while. It's football season you know. Where have you been hiding?"

"Oh, I've been busy with school," Celia replied, not really wanting to tell him about how Felicia wasn't really talking to her anymore. Then again, if she wanted his help she would probably have to tell him everything. With that thought in her mind, Celia took a deep breath and said, "Well, actually, Felicia and I aren't talking right now. Um, I was wondering if you have a few minutes to talk to me."

"Sure, I am just picking up some chips for dinner, but I don't have to be home right away. What's up?" Captain Leathers looked at her curiously.

"Well, it's about Felicia. I'm worried about her," Celia started off.

"Really? I have noticed that she hasn't been around much at the house when I'm there," he observed.

"That doesn't surprise me. She's been hanging with a different group of kids this year. And I'm not saying they are a bad group, just different than from what she normally hung with. The story I hear at school is that she is partying pretty heavy every weekend. And, that is really unlike Felicia. Sure, I would drag her to a party now and then, but she would never drink. The school grapevine is saying that not only is she attending these parties, but she is drinking pretty heavily at them as well."

As Celia told him the rest of the story of how Felicia was acting she felt a sense of relief. Maybe somebody can do something about what was going on. She wanted Felicia's parents to know, which direction Felicia was headed toward, but she knew that if Felicia ever found out what Celia said, she would never be forgiven.

By the time Celia finished her story, Captain Leathers looked very concerned. "I appreciate you telling me about Felicia's behavior. I will talk to her parents tonight when I go over for dinner."

"OK, but promise you won't tell them you heard all this from me. Felicia would never forgive me if she found out I told you what I know," begged Celia.

"Don't worry, Kiddo, I won't tell them. They know I have my resources on finding out information and won't question where the information came from. Thanks again," and with that, Leathers grabbed his favorite lime-flavored tortilla chips and headed toward the cashier.

Celia headed over to the bakery to get the French baguette for their dinner that night, all the while hoping she did the right thing by talking to Captain Leathers. *Well, what's the worst that could happen,* Celia thought to herself, *it's not like Felicia will stop talking to me. She's already done that.*

Chapter 15

Cyrus Leathers arrived at the Morgan's house around 6:00, just in time for dinner. Mary opened the door with a smile on her face. "We are so glad you were able to come over, Cy," Mary greeted him, using his nickname, with a smile and a hug.

"You know I would never miss the chance for some of your good cooking, and a free meal! I brought chips to go with your husband's famous salsa." Cy handed her the bag of chips as he walked inside the house. Taking a deep breath, letting his nose fill with the smells of the different spices he knew exactly what was prepared for dinner. "Ahhh, you made your famous chicken enchiladas and Spanish rice!"

"You have a good sense of smell, Cy. How did you guess that?"

"Years of training, my dear," Cy said giving Mary a wink.

Laughing, Carl walked into the room, "Don't let him fool you, Mary. I told him what we were having earlier today. Well, I don't know about the rest of this family, but I'm starved. Let's head into the dining room to eat."

As Carl led the way, Mary stopped at the foot of the steps and hollered for the kids to come down to join them for dinner. She sent up a little prayer that Felicia would behave herself. She really didn't know what had gotten into her middle child lately.

Felicia came down grudgingly. She hated eating dinner with her family anymore. Everyone was always too serious.

She was glad to see Cy in the dining room; he would liven things up with his jokes.

As she sat at the table, Cy looked at her with a twinkle in his eyes. "Hey, Snickers," he said greeting her with the nickname he had for her ever since she was eleven and ate a whole bag of mini-Snickers.

Grinning back at him, Felicia said, "Hey, Captain Crunch." She knew that name always bugged him. He would complain that he didn't have a gray beard or a funny hat like Captain Crunch did.

Dinner went more smoothly that evening than it had gone in a few weeks. Felicia knew it was because Cy kept everything light-hearted.

Once dinner was over, the adults moved to the living room while Josh and Felicia headed upstairs to do homework. Felicia was at the first step when her father called to her.

"Felicia, I heard progress reports came out today. We haven't seen yours yet. Can you bring them to us, please?"

"Oh, I accidentally left them in my locker. I'll try to remember them tomorrow. But, I can tell you that they were all Bs," Felicia lied.

"Wonderful! Well, bring them home anyway. You know how we like to see the real thing." Her father turned and walked on into the living room, leaving Felicia to head on up the steps to her room.

As the adults settled in the living room, Carl grabbed the remote to turn on ESPN. Cy halted him, "Carl, Mary, I need to talk to you guys about something serious."

Setting the remote down, Carl looked at his friend quizzically. "What's going on? You look really serious."

"Well, I have come into some information that is serious. It seems that Felicia hasn't been all that truthful with you two," Cy explained. "I had an interesting conversation with someone today, who would like to remain anonymous. It seems that Felicia is running with a different crowd this year—a crowd that has a tendency to party pretty heavily. She has been seen at these parties on many occasions since school began, and drinking quite heavily." Cy went on to explain the rest of what Celia had told him. By the time he was finished, Carl was red in the face with anger while Mary looked about ready to cry.

"My poor baby!" Mary cried. "Something must have happened to create this change in her. She used to never lie to us. She has been telling us that she is staying the night at Celia's these past few weekends."

"What in the devil is she thinking?" growled Carl. "Maybe that is the problem, she isn't thinking. I am going to get her down here right this minute and have her explain herself," Carl thundered, getting out of his seat.

"Now hold up, Carl," Cy told him in a soft voice. "If Felicia is hiding something, yelling at her isn't going to make her feel like opening up to you. And at this point, that is what you need the most."

Cy's reasoning seemed to calm Felicia's dad down somewhat. At least the vein in his head didn't look like it was going to burst like Mt. St. Helen's.

"What are we going to do, Carl?" Felicia's mom asked, wringing her hands worriedly.

"Any suggestions, Cy?" Carl asked.

"Well, my first thought is to sleep on it tonight. Don't confront her when you are angry. I've seen too many teens put a wall up between them and their parents when they feel they are on the defensive. Confronting her when you are angry will put her on that defensive. Tomorrow, I would call the school and talk to the counselor and see if her teachers have noticed anything different. I know she probably has different teachers this year than from last, but someone may have noticed something. Then, and only then, would I talk to her. And when you do talk to her, don't go off half-cocked. Try to stay calm. You want her to open up," Cy advised his friends. Over the years in the police force, he had seen too many kids continue down the path that Felicia was headed down just because of the parents' reactions to the decisions their children made. He didn't want to see that happen with Felicia.

At that moment, Cy's cell phone went off. Glancing at the caller *ID* he decided to take the call. "It's the precinct calling," he explained to his friends. A few minutes later, he was off the phone and bidding a good-bye. "I didn't want to leave this early, but it seems that there was a drug bust on a routine traffic stop, and they want me down there."

"Don't worry about it," replied Carl. "We completely understand. Thank you for coming for dinner, and thank you for talking to us about Felicia. We owe you one."

"Don't think anything of it. I love her like she was my own kid." With that last comment, he closed the front door behind him, leaving Carl and Mary to think about all what he said.

"I think we should take his advice and wait until tomorrow," Mary said.

Carl sighed, "I guess you are right. It would probably be better if I waited until I cooled down anyway. Plus, I would like to know what her teachers have to say about her behavior and grades. I get this feeling that if she has been lying to us all this time about where she has been, then she is probably lying about her grades."

"I hope you are wrong in that," replied Mary. "You go ahead and watch what is left of the game. I'm going to do some cleaning. You know how that helps me settle down when I'm upset about something."

"Sounds good. When you finish, come join me in the living room."

"All right, dear," Mary told him. As she began scrubbing the kitchen, the tears began to fall. *What could possibly be going on with my baby girl? And why does she feel she has to lie and not talk to me? What happened to the days when she felt she could tell me everything?*

Chapter 16

The next day, Felicia was sitting in her third hour—English class, doodling on her notebook. They were supposed to be reading *Julius Caesar*, but who wanted to read about a dead guy written by a dead guy? Plus, that Shakespeare dude wrote in weird language and made it difficult for her to read. She would much rather be working on her communication skills through note writing or her artistic abilities by doodling on paper.

The phone in the classroom rang, and as the person on the other end talked, her teacher looked up right at her. Mrs. Harmon hung up the phone saying, "Felicia, Mrs. James in the guidance office would like to see you."

"Great," mumbled Felicia under her breath. "What did I do this time?" She headed down to the guidance office at a snail's pace. She wasn't in any hurry to get there, and the way Felicia saw it, Mrs. James could just sit and wait before getting the chance to talk to her.

Felicia walked into the guidance office and told the secretary that Mrs. James had called her down.

"Yes, dear, have a seat. She will be with you in a moment," the secretary told her.

Felicia sat in one of the seats with her back to the hallway, facing Mrs. James' door, which was oddly closed. Sitting there wondering what this was all about, Felicia began to look around the office. The guidance staff had decorated the office with hanging green plants by the huge windows facing the courtyard of the school. She could tell that they had made an attempt to try to create the feel of home. Rolling her eyes at that thought, as if school could be anything safe and comfortable as her own bedroom, she heard a door open. Bringing herself out of her thoughts, Felicia looked toward the door.

Mrs. James stood in the doorway, smiling at Felicia. "Come on in, Felicia," she said waving her arm as if she was directing traffic in the middle of Times Square.

Felicia strolled in her office and stopped short when she saw her parents sitting there. *Oh, just perfect* she thought. Choosing to sit in Mrs. James' famous "comfy" chair that was in the corner of her office, Felicia flopped down and swung one of her legs over the arm.

"Felicia, you know better than to sit like that. Sit up," her mother admonished her.

"Oh, she's fine," Mrs. James told her mother. "The majority of the kids choose to sit in that chair. It's why I brought it in; so, the teenagers can be comfortable. The other chairs the district provides can be so uncomfortable and restricting." Mrs. James gave Felicia a reassuring smile before going on.

"I'm sure you are wondering why you are here, Felicia," Mrs. James began.

"Yeah, it crossed my mind," Felicia interrupted and receiving stern looks from both of her parents. She discovered that here lately those looks didn't bug her near as much as they used to.

"Well, your parents came in today concerned about you. I pulled your grades and you definitely are not doing as well as you did last year. At this time last year you had a solid 3.7 GPA, whereas right now you have a 2.0, and you are barely hanging on to that. Your parents, as well as myself, are concerned with what is going on."

Mrs. James stopped with that and stared at Felicia, as if she would just immediately begin spilling her guts. Felicia looked over at her parents. Her mom looked like she was about ready to cry while her dad looked like he was a volcano just waiting to explode. Obviously, Mrs. James must have told him to keep a lid on it otherwise he would be ranting and raving like a lunatic right at this moment. Felicia knew that look well and knew he was on that edge.

Felicia just shrugged. "I don't know what you are talking about. I just find school boring is all. Nothing happened and nothing is wrong. Can I go back to class now? Since you pointed out that I'm making miserable grades, isn't it stupid to pull me out of class when I need to be in there learning?"

"See, that is the attitude we were talking about," her father bit out angrily.

"Mr. Morgan, please, becoming angry isn't going to solve anything," admonished Mrs. James. Felicia instantly liked her. Anyone who would stand up to her dad was worth something in her book.

"Felicia," continued Mrs. James, "I have watched you these past four years and have seen you become a confident and high achieving student. Now all of a sudden your grades are slipping, you aren't participating in class or any extracurricular activities, and you keep to yourself for most of the day. Some of your teachers have noticed that you are no longer hanging out with the friends that you used to . . ."

"So, changing friends is now a crime?" interrupted Felicia.

"No, changing friends is not a crime, but it is concerning when the friends you start hanging out with are known to party, and party a lot," replied Mrs. James.

"Sweetheart," her mother spoke for the first time, "I have noticed a change in you at home. You rarely smile and you stay holed up in your room when you are even home. This is unlike you, and we are just really concerned. I want my happy daughter back."

Felicia looked at her mom and saw the tears well up in her eyes. "I'm sorry, Mom, but I don't know if that is possible."

"I was afraid you would say that," her mother responded. "Mrs. James suggested to us, and your father and I agree with her, that you should visit with someone who specially works with teens."

Felicia's opinion of Mrs. James just dropped back down into the negatives. "What??! You want me to talk to some shrink? No way in hell am I going to talk to some stranger about anything, especially when nothing is wrong!" Felicia was shouting at this point, but she didn't care if the whole school heard her.

"Listen here, young lady, that is enough with the language!" her father shouted right back at her. "As long as you live under our roof, you *will* do as we tell you. And furthermore . . ."

"Mr. Morgan, please lower your voice!" Mrs. James interrupted Felicia's father in mid-rant. Turning to look at Felicia she said, "Your parents are right. You do need to speak with someone, even if you don't think you need to. I have the name of someone that I think you will like and can help you out." She handed a beige business card to Felicia's mom and continued, "I think we have covered all that we need to today. Felicia, you are welcome to finish out the day or go home with your parents."

Great thought Felicia *what a choice I've been given. I can either be in hell at home or in hell at school.* "I'll go home," she mumbled, already thinking of how she could just hole herself up in her room.

Felicia sat slumped in the corner of the back seat. With the cooler weather coming on, the leather seats were cold and she brought her knees up to try and warm herself. She felt cold from the inside out. She stared out the window, watching the different hues on the trees pass by in a blur as her dad drove them home. Fall used to be her favorite season. Now, she just didn't care. She assumed her parents would lecture her all the way home, but the car stayed quieter than a graveyard at midnight. Felicia shivered at the thought.

The minute her dad stopped the car in their driveway, Felicia bolted out of the car and into the house, heading toward the safety of her room. She soon found out that her safe haven wasn't to be as safe as she thought. Just as she turned on her stereo, there was a knock on her door. Felicia chose to ignore it, hoping they would just go away. Luck was definitely not with her today.

"Felicia, either open this door or I will personally take it apart," her father said through the closed door.

Felicia gave the door a disgusted look. She knew her dad would take the door off if he had to; he had done it before. She crossed to the door and yanked it open. "There, it is open. Is that all you needed?"

Both of her parents were standing there, staring at her as if she had grown two horns. "Of course that isn't all that we need," her father blustered. "We need to discuss with you about going to talk to a counselor."

"God, not that again! I don't want to talk to anyone. Nothing is wrong! Why don't you believe me?" Felicia felt the walls closing in on her again, felt the need to get out of what used to be the only room she felt safe in. Her chest constricted, making it difficult to breathe. Felicia knew what was coming next; she had had several episodes of panic attacks followed by hyperventilating. She hated it when she hyperventilated; it always made her feel out of control.

"Carl, this isn't the way to handle the situation. Why don't you leave and let me visit with Felicia for a bit," her mom intervened. Much to Felicia's surprise, her father agreed and left them alone.

Her mom softly closed the door as her dad walked out. She turned and softly walked to Felicia's bed and sat down. "Come over here, Sweetheart, and sit with me."

"I'm fine where I am, Mom," Felicia stubbornly said as she sat in her favorite reading chair.

Her mom nodded her head, as if saying that it was OK if Felicia didn't want to sit next to her. "You know, your father and I are really concerned about you. That is why we went in to school today."

"Whatever . . ." Felicia started to say.

"Don't interrupt. Just listen to me for a minute. Can you do that for me?" Her mom asked. Felicia nodded and her mom continued. "I know you feel as if there isn't anything wrong, and you really don't want to talk to anyone. But, I'm asking you to just give it a try. Visit with this counselor that was recommended for four weeks. After that, we won't make you go back if you don't want to."

Felicia thought about the offer. *Four weeks isn't that long of a time,* she thought. "Do you promise to leave me alone ifI go for that long and then quit?" Felicia knew that the one thing she could count on was that her mom always kept her promises. If Mary Morgan used the word "promise" in a sentence, she would hold to it.

"I promise that I or your father will not make you continue seeing the counselor if you want to quit after four weeks," her mom said looking right into her eyes.

Felicia saw the truth there. She knew her mom could get her dad to do whatever she wanted. But still, she didn't want to commit to anything. The thought of talking to anyone, especially a stranger, made her feel as if another panic attack was about to start.

"Can I think on it first?" Felicia asked.

"I think that is a fair request," her mom responded. "Sleep on it tonight and let us know tomorrow. I'm going to head downstairs and get dinner out of the freezer. I'm making my famous chicken and dumplings tonight." Her mom stood up and walked over to where Felicia was sitting. "I'll call you down when dinner is ready." She leaned forward and gave Felicia a kiss on her forehead and then headed out of the room.

Felicia never made it down for dinner. After her mom left the bedroom, Felicia went over to her bed and curled up with her favorite bear. She laid there with thoughts tumbling through her mind. *Should I talk to someone? What if all they do is remind me of how stupid I was? What if I tell her everything and she just laughs or worse tell me all these fears are in my head?* With that last thought, Felicia fell asleep.

Chapter 17

Six months later

It was a bright, crisp morning with the sun shining and small wispy clouds were high in the sky. Felicia was walking Josh to his soccer game. Once they reached the park, Josh ran off to join his team, and Felicia decided to look for a swing to sit in and wait for him to be done.

Finding a swing set not too far from the game, Felicia sat and pushed herself off the ground. She loved to swing; it made her feel free and without a care in the world. As she kept climbing higher and higher, she let her thoughts drift over the past six months.

She finally agreed to talk with the counselor, Carol, who she discovered was actually a pretty nice person and easy to talk to. She never laughed at Felicia's fears and gave her some techniques on how to handle the panic attacks. She learned to take slow deep breaths to help control hyperventilating, which also helped her feel more in control of herself.

There had been more storms blow over the area during this time, and each storm seemed less threatening. Felicia found herself consoling Josh during one particular lightening storm. Through all of the loud snaps of lightening striking the surrounding trees and ground, and the house shaking booms that followed, Felicia didn't jump, didn't run for her room to sit curled up in a ball, and even left her bear sitting on the shelf. Instead she talked with Josh about his fear of the storm—never making fun of him. Felicia discovered as she talked with Josh, soothing him with reassuring words, that she began to believe those words herself and the storms seemed less frightening.

The four weeks had come and gone and Felicia decided to continue to talk with Carol, talking about the many secrets she kept locked up inside. She had been visiting with her for six months now. One day, about three months ago, Felicia told her the biggest secret she kept, the story of Jeff and what happened that last day she saw him. She heard many adults talking in the past how girls put themselves in the position of being assaulted or even raped. It never bothered her until that fateful day, and then it made her angry. Carol sat listening to Felicia tell her story, explain her fear of being watched and Carol never laughed, never called her stupid, and most importantly never told her that it was her fault. In fact, much to Felicia's surprise, Carol insisted that it was not her fault at all. As Carol explained it, Felicia began to realize that Jeff should have respected her enough to listen to her as she said "no." She was still trying to grasp the idea that the assault wasn't her fault, and the more she told herself that the more she believed it. She was worth being respected for her values. Felicia decided over the past three months that if a guy didn't respect her for who she was then he was not worth giving the time of day to. She was worth waiting for and she knew that someday a guy would realize that.

She and Celia were talking again. Felicia hadn't realized how much she had missed talking to her best friend until they began talking again. She still hadn't told Celia about the assault, but knew that one day she would. It wasn't that she was afraid Celia would make fun of her, tell her she was being a baby about it all; Celia had her own problems to handle at the moment. Felicia wasn't sure what was going on, but she could tell in Celia's voice when they talked that something was up. At school she could tell that Celia was pre-occupied with something. While Felicia wanted to help her best friend, she wanted to concentrate on getting better first.

She wasn't going to parties anymore and concentrated on her schoolwork instead. Felicia realized that she hadn't had a drink in over four months. Her grades were coming up and while she wouldn't graduate with honors like she had hoped, she was proud of her achievements.

Felicia realized that she had slowed down her swinging as her thoughts had drifted. She jumped off the swing and headed over to watch Josh's game. As she walked, Felicia noticed that she no longer felt as though someone was lurking behind a tree or building, watching, and waiting. She was beginning to feel confident, this time truly confident and not the fake confidence she used to portray to her friends. Smiling, she tilted her face to the sun, and for the first time began to think of her future. She would be graduating soon and going to college. *Without any of the secrets,* Felicia thought, *I feel as if I can do and achieve anything.* And with that thought, and a lighter heart, she jogged over to the game to cheer her little brother on.

Author's Note

Felicia's story is not an uncommon one; however, it is one that is not told by many teens or young women. According to the National Crime Victimization Survey conducted by the U.S. Department of Justice, in 1996, teens sixteen to nineteen were three and one-half times more likely than the general population to be victims of rape, attempted rape, or sexual assault. The 2007 survey shows that there were about 248 to 300 sexual assaults in the United States. While 44 percent of assaults and rape victims are under the age of eighteen, 80 percent are under the age of thirty with college age women being four times more likely to be assaulted.

Unfortunately, sexual assault is one of the least reported crimes. Around 60 percent of the crimes go unreported.

Many women, and especially men, do not report this type of crime. Young women can feel responsible for the assault, like Felicia did in the story. According to Schwartz and Legget, one-fourth of all college age rape victims blame themselves entirely for the attack.[1]

Sexual assaults can have devastating effects on the victims. The victims can suffer depression, post traumatic stress disorder (PTSD), or have more of tendency to drink alcohol and take drugs, as well as contemplate suicide. It is

---

[1]   Schwartz, M. Leggett, M. Bad Dates, Emotional Trauma—the Aftermath of Campus Sexual Assault—Violence Against Women, Vol. 5, No. 3, March, 1999.

important for the victim to receive professional help. More information on statistics, the effects, and recovering from the assault can be found at *http://www.rainn.org*. All of the statistics reported in this book come from this Web site, in which their information was obtained from reliable sources including U.S. Bureau of Justice Statistics, U.S. Department of Justice, and World Health Organization.

Get Published, Inc!
Thorofare, NJ 08086
10 March, 2010
BA2010069